This vast world, so many stories; all the lives they had read, heard, conferred and shared together. Tales that stayed connected to them tight like shadows. The Lyra and Wills, Heathcliff, Moriarty, the Bennets, Alice, Montagus, Lolita, Dracula, Poirot, Smiley, a Pip or a Rhett, a Tinkerbell, a Moll or an Atticus, all of them familiar and sacred. Each book leaving a residue behind inside those readers like a new memory between them, building up, every story adding to it, each new script, creating their own internal memoir notes; a library of two; kept soft and secret behind their eyes.

They thought themselves safe hiding between the endless piles, the shelves of wanted themed collections and tender first editions, that nestled amongst the hardbacks, the paperbacks, the fonts, the quotes, the titles and chapters, every single written line somehow they would be unharmed under this loving literary protection.

How could they have guessed their own plot that awaited them? Had they not learned from all those great fictitious characters and glorious imagined events that life was never so clear, so beautiful or kind to two young people as in love as anyone outside of books had ever been.

If they had just considered the fates of Daisy and Gatsby once his infamous parties had ceased and the green light stilled; recalled the plight of Almasy and Katharine after carrying her over that dry desert end, her last message to him composed; to please remember such a fierce and frightening War, when Andrei finally lay in his Natasha's care needing more time; would they have been prepared? Could they have been? Could anyone?

Stories, every one of us: whether a comedy, a tragedy, significant or memorable; unknown in length, the depth of our journeys or the very time of its ending.

Stories, that's what this is, that's what they are: that language, our verses, those chronicles of life. Tales told with words. It must, of course, come down to words, those fearless, enthralling, revealing terms and expressions, those very things that made their brains sing and their hearts burn up. For those two it was forever and absolutely always about the words.

Words.   With.   Love.   X

Chapter One

"The reading of all good books is like a conversation
with the finest minds of past centuries."
Rene Descartes

After

"Ladies and Gentleman, thank you so very much for taking time out of your busy lives and coming along to the twentieth anniversary of the esteemed Oxford Festival of Books. It has been an incredible journey to see how over those years this fledgling event has expanded and spiralled outwards and upwards, practically touching the university spires and gargoyles themselves. Evolving from a handful of local bookshops and borrowed university lecture rooms it is now a colossal three day event playing host to more than ten thousand visitors over thirty five historical venues across our stunning city.

In honour of this prestigious anniversary we would like to open this year's Festival with the session we have titled 'In Conversation with Ed Williams.' He is one of the most celebrated Author, Editor and Publishers active today with a career spanning three decades and counting."

An embarrassed cough and shake of the head from the gentleman sitting quietly in the armchair on the unlit stage behind, was noted by the five hundred capacity audience seated in the benches all round him. This caused a murmur of laughter from many which made the speaker at the auditorium podium pause for a beat, good-humouredly.

"His books on both C.S. Lewis and F. Scott Fitzgerald, have been on the A Level curriculum for over eighteen years. His compilations of English and American Poetry have been on UK best seller lists for as long as I have been able to read. He has mentored in his twenty five year service at Fallon Publishing House, too many successful writers to mention individually here. Indeed many of them have been our most popular and fastest sold-out guest speakers at this very festival in recent times. Despite his unquestionable Oxfordshire roots I understand even Cambridge will confirm they have heard of him." At this the armchair man joined in with the chuckling surrounding him.

"I doubt there is a Man Booker, ABA or Noble prize nominee he hasn't read, met or invited to his legendary 'Wilde' monthly lunch table at the London Claridges Hotel." Stage whispering now he continued, "It's wonderful. I've been along three times! Have the monkfish."

"Perhaps not a fourth…" muttered the guest into his shirt microphone causing again a ripple of laughter throughout the esteemed building; its enormous domed ceiling catching the happy acoustics and bouncing it back beneath it and all around.

"He has worked for many years promoting childhood literacy in schools as well as visiting foreign countries with Oxfam, building libraries and book shelters across the third world devastated by War, Diseases and Famine. This has generated over a million young fiction paperbacks so far, being donated by ongoing sponsorships. In his recent talks with the Government Charities Committee, Ed referred to the Lewis insight of 'Since it is likely that children will meet cruel enemies, let them at least have heard of brave knights and heroic courage', to explain why books have such importance to this cause. How books can, not simply delight and educate these youthful minds through the imagination of fiction, myths, even magic but hopefully offer the chance to encourage, improve and overcome their situations in the face of such devastating conditions and experiences we here could never understand."

It was silent around the room with honoured reverence. The speaker concluded.

"Awarded an OBE for services to Literature earlier this year, with the promise he will never, ever write his autobiography, which will have those Claridges visitors no doubt mopping their brows with great relief. It is my enormous privilege to present to you all here today…Mr Ed Williams."

Spotlight now on, the audience clapped loudly as the atmosphere within the venue buzzed with genuine excitement. The speaker, Marcus Hollier, walked over to the free chair on the stage behind, pausing first to lean over to Ed and warmly shake the outstretched hand with both of his; familiar and respectful. Ed smiled up at him, his gentle grey eyes creased kindly at their corners. His seated, cross legged body language displayed no sign of any nervousness as he rested his elbows onto the plush chair arms. A small navy book perched on his lap, a pair of closed reading glasses sat upon it.

He looked smart in his dark suit and white shirt, unbuttoned once at the neck, no tie. His sandy coloured hair was cut short but thick in texture, giving him a youthful appearance, perhaps a decade or so less than his fifty-one years. He certainly looked in good physical shape for someone who, by his own admission, sat down not moving for almost all of the hours in the day and possibly most of the night ones too. His 'Reading is only exercise for the brain, not the body – unfortunately' had been a popular quotation taken from him in recent years, and enjoyed by the youthful online masses.

Sitting there in the magnificent hallowed hall, one of his most favourite monuments of architecture in the entire country, Ed couldn't help but recall being in this same city twenty years before. It was the day that meant more to him than any other in his whole life; the day that changed the course of his own world forever.

How often when recalling the precise memory on that exceptional morning fear would take hold of him sharply like a brittle wind. That terror of the 'what if's' that can frighten each person if they thought too much about anything historically; to consider the concept of Fates, coincidence, to reflect on Robert Frost's *Two Roads*. Some days Ed agonised how if he had decided not to answer that letter inviting him here, if Paul had not taken charge to organise a meeting, if his train had not been late, that old lady... so many factors that could have meant he never saw *her*. Of all the people living in the same planet that he would never know, no reason ever to meet, perhaps she could have been one of them. An involuntary shudder went down his spine and he blinked to try and force it away. His Izzy. The tale of their lives. The most important story he could never read.

"...I'll love you, dear, I'll love you
  Till China and Africa meet
  And the river jumps over the mountain
  And the salmon sing in the street.

  I'll love you till the ocean
  Is folded and hung out to dry
  And the seven stars go squawking
  Like geese about the sky..."

As I Walked Out One Evening, W.H. Auden

Chapter Two

"...Two circles that touched. But those two circles, above all point at which they touched, are the very thing I am mourning for, homesick for famished for. You tell me 'she goes on'. But my heart and body are crying out, come back, come back. Be a circle touching my circle on the plane of Nature. But I know this is impossible. I know that the thing I want is exactly the thing I can never get."

A Grief Observed, C.S. Lewis

After

She lay under the warm covers, consciousness starting to rouse her from the heavy, dreamless sleep the drugs had induced. For those few seconds she felt at peace. She lay there enjoying the body heat that the blankets contained, safe and enveloping. Her head turned to the left side of the bed to see him. The profile of the one she knew so well. Looking now she could see his brow tightened and his eyes crinkled up softly the way he would look whenever he was sad. His breathing was slightly ragged and tight, like someone who had been trying to quietly contain their crying so as not to wake another, perhaps sleeping close by. His broad shoulders sagged lowly with the weight of his pain.

Izzy saw this and her morning fog of confusion immediately cleared into sharp focus. Seeing him so upset she remembered. The steady, hard spear of a fragmented blade travelling slowly down into her chest was hot and definite. She could feel the sensation of the scraping out of flesh in all of the corners from the top of her belly to the deepest parts of her aching, empty womb. And she remembered. And it was all evident again. The physical pain from loss; the actual bodily agony of grief that was as real as any man made weapon could cause upon and under her skin; bright, burning, deserving.

He sensed she was awake now and straightened himself out as if he could iron away all the hurt he hadn't realised she had already seen. Like a soldier, he held himself together, defiant and steady, before he gently pushed his bed-crumpled head further down onto his pillow and turned to face her, so close that their noses almost touched. His breath against her lips, his calm grey eyes searching hers.

Izzy looked at him deeply. Desperate to explain, to tell him in all the words she knew, what it felt like on the very insides of her. Not just the soreness, but the full want of their missing child. She had so many thoughts and ideas filling up inside her head and needing so much to share them with him, to ask him simple questions, like a child herself. Her eyes brimmed up full with tears that had yet to fall as he watched her, not knowing what to do, how to help this woman he had so much love for. The one he vowed to look after and protect, so aware he, at this moment, wasn't accomplishing either of those things.

And he looked at her as though she was a tiny, fragile bird made of fine glass, hanging high on a piano wire. His heart raced at the thought of her not staying up, that the weight inside the shape was too much for the wire to hold on to. It was precariously placed above a well, an old dark open well, that when you looked close enough, was a huge black hole without end; that if she fell into it, there could be no return, just a continuous falling, alone and frightening. He couldn't reach that bird so high above. There was no way of catching it before it fell down without stretching too far and falling with it into that deep, dark beyond.

Ed looked at her. He looked back into her eyes, as deep as that well, and kissed her. He knew of nothing else to do. Helpless and afraid, he carefully kissed her as if it would tell her how much he adored her. How sorry he was; how desperately he wanted that fragile bird, so much, not to fall.

Izzy's eyes shut briefly as their lips touched, allowing the many tears that she had held in, fall silently down her cheeks and onto the soft pillow they shared. Leaning forward into him, he effortlessly moved his body to mirror her own. His right arm stretched out to pull her close into his aching chest. Her ear pressed down onto his heavy, almost-broken heart, as she stayed there for as long as she dared, listening, listening, to the ever beautiful drumming of that familiar heartbeat.

They lay under the heavy cloud of silence, for as long as they could, lost together. Their wordlessness, like a gentle breeze, steadily rocking that small, glass bird back and forth over the abyss.

"I have learned now that whilst those who speak about one's miseries usually hurt, those who keep silence hurt more."

C. S. Lewis

Chapter Three

"A book is the only place you can examine a fragile thought without breaking it."
Edward P. Morgan

After

The Sheldonian Theatre, although filled to capacity, was absolutely silent. The audience, some with pens poised and notebooks ready, a few with camera phones recording this momentous talk, others leaning forward on the padded folded out front chairs or on the smooth dark wooden benches that curved across the enormous apex in the higher rows. Every person different yet joined together in their fevered interest on this much-publicised new theory, their curiosity and attention peaked to hear the explanation from such a reverential man justify this original, exciting notion in his seminal work.

Marcus Hollier sat opposite Ed on the raised stage. They both had their microphones tucked into the jacket lapels so they could talk in a more relaxed fashion than the old way of hand held mics. Over the many years of their friendship they had sat in similar seated positions, facing each other and engaging in long and passionate discussions about Books and Publishing. What constituted a great read: Who were their favourite Authors and why: What is the absolute definition of a good story: Why Literature is resolutely important; Hardbacks over Paperbacks: Printed copies versus eCopies and so much more. It essentially was an infinite area of thoughts and ideas going back and forth. Many times there were no right answers simply expressed personal opinions formed from a whole history of reasons, plenty of evenings they would try and persuade or deter the other from a decision they felt recklessly ill-considered, there were even occasions when they would agree on something.

Two friends who enjoyed dissecting and embracing this world of language and tales they, like so very many others, felt such a strong urge to discover and protect.

"Ed, firstly congratulations of your new book, your eighth I believe. All of them have been non-fiction and this particular read seems to be different to your previous publications. In the past you have authored Biographies, Literary Criticisms and Compilations on your preferred Poets and Writers across the centuries but this recent edition, *Wysten's Words*, seems to contain more of a personal dialogue, a stronger sense of yourself and your opinion about the world. Does that seem fair?" Marcus lent back slightly to allow the question to hang between them for a moment. He had been as interested as everyone attending there today as to Ed's answer.

"Yes Marcus," Ed replied. "I do feel this book has a much bigger sense of self than any of the others. It is the most autobiographical I ever intend to get."

"The papers in recent months have clung on to that very engaging headline, using the quote on your front cover, 'Words to Save Your Life'. Could you please expand on this for us."

Marcus settled in for the start of Ed's careful and thoughtful reply, so happy others now within that wondrous building could share in the brilliance of this man: his vibrant and energetic intellect on matters, his joy of thought and life-learning, so reflective of his big, beautiful nature.

"Words matter. Words change your life. Make it better, happier. Feed your fears or quell your beasts. They can ruin your life. They can save your life. Words are here to show our primal, human desperate need to communicate and to belong with others. To expel and translate to another being the noises that pervades our private minds. They are perhaps the most important things we have the power to own or control. They are both dangerous weapons and maternal comfort.

If we think of what happens in our life, how we are able to get across what we desire, it is language that enables us to achieve this. However, I am not here to discuss the origin of speech and variety of tongues and tones, signing and codes available to us, there are many others who are much more qualified scientifically and technically about such things. What I would like to examine for a moment is the reason of why we use language, how we use it and to what avail. The ancient storytelling, the angry prostrations, the loving proposals, the anguish of expressing loss; all of these are relevant to shaping human conditions, to educate, inform and confer.

I have witnessed a grown man walk back from a roof top he had climbed with the purpose of jumping off it to his death because of a young policeman talked him safely down.

I have heard political of speeches by Kennedy, Hitler, Lenin, Churchill, which inspired and braced entire nations to conform to and willingly defend with their own lives, ideas and decisions made by another. '…We shall go on to the end, we shall fight in France, we shall fight on the seas and oceans, we shall fight with growing confidence and growing strength in the air, we shall defend our Island, whatever the cost may be…would carry on the struggle, until, in God's good time, the New World, with all its power and might, steps forth to the rescue and the liberation of the old.'

A King's abdication was transmitted over the radio waves with the confession he 'found it impossible to carry the heavy burden of responsibility and to discharge my duties as King as I would wish to do without the help and support from the woman I love.' Using heartfelt words to clarify how he gave up the absolute obligation and purpose he was born into, for a woman deemed unsuitable for the affiliate role. He *told* us so.

I have listened to a child stop crying, even though he remained in pain, only because he had heard his mother comforting soft lines whispered into his tiny ear. People have fired bullets out of guns into other human beings in response to painful announcements or aggressive threats fired out as words from their mouths. You do not marry another without still, at first, asking.

You may well demonstrate with body language and thoughtful gestures, how much you care about another but it is not until you say those three words, those eight small letters that changes the dynamic between two previous hesitant individuals that makes more of a future impact than anything else. I. Love. You.

The closest couples I know use a repeated section of words to exclude others and create a private aural place just for them. It is impossible to underestimate the importance of words. The spoken word, language can be from impulsive and emotional to considered and persuasive.

However to make the biggest impact, the talking we do is for the most part, unfiltered, spontaneous and trivial. Of course it is, it should be. Conversations can't all be brain-aching and deeply meaningful, we'd be exhausted or all go mad. So if we agree to this point we must concede that only a fraction of speech is profound and insightful enough to remember. Writing speeches is clearer and "better" than speaking as it is edited in its intentions. Its conciseness is its power. Yes I absolutely believe words can change your life, how could they not. What is more interesting is perhaps how they can save it…"

The audience murmured amongst themselves at the final statement. Marcus Hollier nodded his head towards Ed in a gesture that gave finality in the answer of his initial question. It was the equivalent to a motionary full stop.

"In Ireland, novels and plays still have a strange force. The writing of fiction and the creation of theatrical images can affect life more powerfully and stealthily than speeches, or even legislation. Imagined worlds can lodge deeply in the private sphere, dislodging much else, especially when the public sphere is fragile."

Colm Toibin

Chapter Four

"You are the finest, loveliest, tenderest and most beautiful person I have ever known –

And even that is an understatement."

F. Scott Fitzgerald

Before

I love her. I always have. It was the simplest thing in the world to want to be with her and only her. There was no choice or competition. No confusion or distraction. I love her. All of her. Her beautiful mind, her phenomenal body. I fell in love with every wonderful flying spark that burst inside of her mind and showered them out into the colours of her eyes.

In my youth I might have imagined a Goddess from the myths, a Diana, Hera or Athena, full of power and sexual charge. Later I wondered if that had even been possible, what we would have even talked about? Body beauty aside I learned very quickly that it was the wonder of the mind that would always entice me above all other. The seduction of the intellect which would win me over hands down.

I had hoped from my future companion, a kindness, a certain sense of gentleness so I could feel at peace with the world. I never had any time for high drama or game play. For me, they were things saved for the theatre boards and rugby fields.

Twenty years ago I had my world changed by meeting a woman of such importance to me that I felt breathless as to know how to keep her. I had no experience enough to charm her to me or impress her with romantic confidence. Yet somehow I found a way, a book of course was the clue. It always was. It was always going to be this path.

"You are mysterious.

I love you.

You're beautiful, intelligent and virtuous,

And that's the rarest known combination."

F. Scott Fitzgerald

Chapter Five

> "Nothing is with me now but a sound
>
> A heart's rhythm, a sense of stars
>
> Leisurely walking around, and both
>
> Talk a language of motion
>
> I can measure but not read:"
>
> W. H. Auden 'Compline'

After

Izzy looked across at her husband and without fully understanding why a spiky sense of irritation rose up from inside her and reached far into the depths of her mind, like a spilt ink well. He had done nothing wrong and she knew this, she really did, in that curved part of her brain that retained rationalisation and perspective, but it was that very crucial region she also noticed which was rapidly closing down.

His large, once-soft and caring hands looked to her, brittle and rough. His ever loving gaze she understood now as quietly judgemental and cold. All the minute, kind gestures and caring signs he once gave her now felt sodden and dripping with blame; *her* broken body, *her* inferior maternity, *her* inability to keep their child growing safe inside.

Ed said nothing of this of course. None of it had never even entered his head, but she projected her pain as if it emerged correctly translated from his thoughts and didn't consider asking his confirmation. The fact Ed did nothing to correct her dark and vicious accusations, even though he had not been informed of them, mattered little to her. All her brain could manage was fuelled by the hormones that overtook her. Their baby died. His part was done, ticked off at the conception so all he needed was sit back and wait nine months until she completed her role; much harder and more complex, of course, but solely her responsibility, there was nothing else he could do.

The effort for Izzy to form speech, actual words and letters in her mouth seemed too exhausting to create so she lay on the long chair festering like an open wound that couldn't help but incite any dangerous germs floating invisibly around to come nearer and risk infection. Her swollen breasts ached dully with the milk that couldn't come out, heavy and trapped. She welcomed the discomfort. The drugs that the hospital doctor prescribed placed her in the fuzzy limbo of the world, unable to see straight, think clearly or feel entirely the low draw on her womb, emptying, slowly and steadily, like a broken ship leaking out into the oceanic void its once precious treasure.

How different hours make. Ninety-one of them ago they were the picture of happiness, the ideal poster of two excited adults in love, enjoying the willing expansion of their family. He was the protector and she the provider, locked in their safe bubble that their love created. As they walked hand in hand along Magdalen Street in the early afternoon, muted sunshine and autumn warm, enjoying the people-watching of students, tourists and shoppers, they did not know what was going to happen in less than a minute's time.

How if they had been told, would that have made it better or worse? Do you lose your happiness when you know the thing you desperately want will be unfairly snatched away or are you happier because you still have it there at that very moment even though it will not last? Like a scythe that cuts through time and leaves a rip into the pavement you once trod, you can see your life before where you carried on oblivious, heading towards home and then crossed over it to that moment you could feel you were bleeding. How you cannot rush back to those spaces where you once stood, before that tear, because you never can. No matter how hard your heart wills it or your mind pulls against the next stage like an anguished toddler, you know that once that moment in time has been cut open, you are eternally a different person; it is unsalvageable.

Time now becomes a very definite framework of three, your past, present and future. The past, one minute before, was those pavement slabs where you innocently walked on, then the fearful slice upon which creates your present, a frightening sensation when you stop having reached over the gap and into the now where your body isn't doing what it is supposed to and the end result of this is feared but not yet known. Three hours later, in that future, your nightmare is confirmed and you are powerless to change the very outcome you would never have chosen.

That first pavement part was walked on together by three people, three heartbeats, three lives; two larger and one very small and yet in that fragment of time crossing over that line, when Izzy had begun to feel that dampness and aching cramp, only two heartbeats were left. These stages of moments would always matter to them now. Their forever selves having a marker of what they would remember as *before* and *after*. What was yet unknown, was the next part, *future*. How could they ever recover? How could they ever possibly feel the love and happiness, the completion of their perfect union again? Would it have been better to never have known that first parental joy? Was having those three heartbeats between them for as long as they had, worth the loss of only remaining as two?

Izzy now looked across at where Ed was. The fore shadow of presumed judgement she painted him with made her feel nauseous and weak. She could see him sitting down on the couch they once shared together. The missing space of her shape next to his felt obvious to them both, his tinged with sadness, hers with spite, as he leant back with the four printed manuscripts heavy on his lap.

Ed's eyes looked over to the chaise longue opposite, to try and find Izzy's, but she didn't return it, her guilt made her lowered eyelids too heavy to lift. Instead she focussed on the paper pages he had on him, wondering for a short while what stories they might contain, what other lives they could be describing, away from this hateful present, this lonesome grief. Soon she stopped caring about the undiscovered books and tilted her head back to stare up at the blank, white ceiling as she wished all her thoughts away. What she wanted was that solitary, silent place where she could exist without feelings, blame or hope, especially Hope. That was the one that stung the most today; she feared that always would.

The space between them both in their small but comfortable front room was no more than three metres apart but it might well have been the miles of the vast Atlantic Ocean, soundless and still. Ed sunk into his new story gratefully. He shamefully felt momentary relief in distracting himself from the horrors of this past week they both had endured. Unknown in how he could continue his helplessness and anguish, to try and repair or fix his heartbroken wife. All Ed felt he could now achieve was perhaps a quiet chance at respite with those anonymous written stories, before he could gain the internal strength to start tomorrow with some idea of easing her.

Ed began reading the handwritten notes Carron had neatly made based on her cursory read through; mentally recording key words like *emotive subject, raw characters* and *intriguing third person voice* before carefully folding it over to begin his own first read. This was one of Ed's very favourite things to do. The startle of a fresh author's work, the visceral exhilaration he felt in holding an unknown piece of writing and the pure joy of unfolding and indulging into another's entirely original world. He knew that for the next few hours he would be lost, engrossed deep and far away from the reality of actual life. Absorbing himself into the possible and allowing himself to feel hopeful, always so full of hope, in case these stories, these yet unpublished pieces, the work of dedicated talents, could be something of literary outstanding.

The glass bird shone bright above them in the moonlight, haunting and noiseless watching the two figures so quiet, so separate, beneath.

"Hope is the thing with feathers

That perches in the soul,

And sings the tune without words

And never stops at all.

The sweetest in the gale is heard

And sore must be the storm

That could abash the little bird

That kept so many warm.

I've heard it in the chilliest land

And on the strangest sea;

Yet never in extremity

It asked a crumb from me."

Emily Dickinson

Chapter Six

"There seems to be hardly any one among my acquaintance from whom I have not learned."

The Allegory of Love, C. S. Lewis

Before

Ed liked it best being together those evening on his battered brown leather couch. Izzy would lie softly across two thirds of it, her legs draping gently across his lap as he sat back happily, one arm resting warmly over her shins.

Ed watched Izzy as her fingers whitened slightly as both hands gripped the book's pages tighter. He leant his head up a fraction to see her beautiful, sweet face darkened and frowning, those cautious green eyes darting quickly over, across and down the page inhaling the story at a frenetic pace. Had he reached for her wrist pulse he would have surely felt the urgency of its increased beating, reacting in symmetry with how her brain was absorbing the peaking of the tale. Her physical body breathless, tense and aflame echoing her emotional response, nervous and full of anxious anticipation to uncover the final answers for the characters and their end-journey this author had decided to disclose.

The coffee table in front of them looked as if divided into two halves. On the left side sat his piles of manuscripts, an amount some nights that could be as many as twelve but never fewer than four. Beside these pages were his 'tools', three arrow point sharpened 2B pencils placed parallel to his trusted black Lamy biro pen, along with one leather bound, lined paged notebook.

In between these two personal territories would be an opened bottle of good red wine: A wine chosen together from any of their lazy weekend wanders around the city's specialist food markets or intimate family run stores, always after long discussions on their merits and origins. Ed and Izzy would each ask and listen, hearing the history of the country it came from, understanding a little more each time about the differing processes or grape variety that the labels represented. Talking and deciding as a team they indulged themselves with appreciation of the deep, rich-red liquid they so enjoyed. They wanted to savour each complex element, unique fragrances and flavours, sharing in these little moments of daily gratitude and celebration together: Purposefully. Their two half-full glasses of equal volumes within arms-reach, were perched neatly in front of the large grey bowl resting beautifully behind them, glasses waiting to be sipped and enjoyed with this fresh tradition they had started.

Over to the far right edge of the table, Izzy's side, was a pile of carefully selected book of all genres, publications and writers. These could range from dusty, last mid-century American poetry, a mountain of old orange and cream colour-blocked Penguin classics most often re-reads, a list of biographies of any person someone had considered worthy to author, an alarmingly eye-catching collection of science fiction novellas with planet painted covers all resting upon the latest books on the best seller lists from either side of the Atlantic.

As a world-known Literary Agent and Publisher held in wide regard, over the year Ed would be sent the full selection of the titles from the up and coming book awards. This was always a great source of delight and excitement from them both.

Each of their two spaces had books upon them that were forever changing, read, remembering, exchanging, replacing. Ed preferred to read his work stories he took home from the office in the front room as he snatched those extra after supper hours to keep working on unseen pieces. This meant he saved the published novels for his own quiet time. These consisted of daily readings on his early morning commute to work on the train; within that one-way fifty minute travel he could easily finish a whole novella or using both the start and end ride of this journey, complete a regular size paperback novel well enough to remember every chapter in depth.

In his bedroom in the week days Ed would divert himself into the large tower of newly-released hardbacks ever present by his bedside for a while longer before he went to sleep. Or he would take both the Saturday and Sunday, finding long spaces of time in the front room, their small back City garden, weather allowing, in a long, hot bath or on their regular walks out and about snatching moments when Iz would rest with him on a park bench, or sit listening to the live music bands in the cafes and bars on a hot afternoon.

Ed's most favourite time was when she would ask him to read parts to her, out loud, just the two of them. She would settle into him like a soft scarf and lie still. Her arms wrapped lightly around, holding him close. One hand would rest upon his upper left chest. She liked to feel how his heart worked whilst his deep, gentle speech breezed over her hair, down her forehead and into her willing ears. Listening to him tell a story, any type of one, any part of it, was to sense absolute joy. How he took the page and made it come alive and as true as if they were actually walking together, existing in those descriptions on the page.

On the occasions when Izzy would later unintentionally pick out this same book from their stacks at home to read it herself, always when she reached the part that Ed's voice had touched, she would slow everything down and remember each line, almost each syllable and letter of his pronouncing. Those surprising moments felt something as perfect as pure magic. She could hardly breathe with the miracle of it.

In my head I heard your telling of Alice Timble's Autobiography, Chapter Five this morning; bringing to life the remembrance of her foster parents speaking at her wedding. How you had robustly described, from her own wondrous words, those funny anecdotes her Scottish foster father recalled, those numerous childhood mishaps which had me laughing out loud, (even though I was alone), all over again. But afterwards, balanced a few pages later in your quieter, tender tone was the inclusion of her elderly foster mother's sweet quotation from a letter Alice had written to them when she finally left their home to travel. How I wept at the simple, honest gratitude she extolled, and how because of them, she described feeling her life had been truly saved.

I would have loved that Chapter anyway. It was so exquisitely written. Yet for me, because it was from you the first time I knew of it, because that incredible event was spoken to me so gently, with an understanding of text and meaning only you can convey, I loved it so very much more: More, more, unquestionably so.

Not having my parents at our own wedding was of course hard for me. Listening to you tell a tale of another, a sad child turned around with love, meant I understood her world for those few minutes, just snatching a little time from her shared truths, and it made my heart sing. You made me see another's occasion and I have learnt, as ever, I have learnt and understood just a small part of what something magnificent was to her. Thank you. Truly, I thank you, for I know I live my own singular life but with reading myself, even more so with hearing your narration, so close and vivid, I feel I live a hundred lives yet remain by your side.

I.

Love.

You. X

"I have always imagined that paradise will be a kind of library."

Jorge Luis Borges

Chapter Seven

"But in reading great literature I become a thousand men and yet remain myself."

C.S. Lewis

After

Ed continued to answer Marcus at the Sheldonian.

"It could be said that due my impressive education and wider literary knowledge, or perhaps to the detriment of it, I could write you a thousand essays on the meaning of Love over the centuries. I could quote Milton and Browning, I could speak one hundred sonnets on that very subject. I had read Shakespeare so many times it felt some days we were brothers, and that familial bond meant I could recognise how and where this passion would arise from all the characters that walked on his stage. More examples, from Heathcliff to Darcy, to Anthony and Cleopatra, Romeo and Juliet, even the sparing drunk couples in Albee and Williams's plays, I knew of Love…theoretically. I discussed, devoured and dissected its inner workings to the point of putting all the pieces back together again like a cuckoo clock.

What I did not understand yet was the practical part beyond the page, how to implement in the real world such emotional and romantic connections. As an only child to elderly parents, no close cousins to speak of that could widen my social skills; I was the cliché of therapists' scripts. With my Boys boarding education until my university years at Oxford where, despite girls being included in my new college life, they remained as foreign to me as the newly discovered species that Lord Attenbourgh enthrals us all with on BBC1. My youthful, hormonal spirit was willing yet the brain was still catching up, as if lost on a train towards mid-Europe, mid-century even, whilst my gangly, awkward body stood firmly in the fine streets of central England, anxious and aloof.

Work was a god-send. It kept me busy, happy and honest. It was always more than simply a Career; it was a heartfelt yearning to be involved in every aspect of Literature, a genuine fascination of genres and writers, my definitive obsession. To be paid for, and be hopefully making a personal, worthwhile difference in the subject I so adored, was a dream role for me. I still cannot believe my luck. The old slogan of 'if you love what you do you never have to work a day in your life' had never felt more astute.

The Publishing Industry has many similar background stories, but thankfully also in the business there was now a regular reason to interact with other people, up and coming, older and wiser, established and satirical, and all those in between. From Beat poets to Austen fanzine editors, Great War biographers to Humorous quotation compilers, I met them all and it was exhilarating, each worthy in their own field and every one joined by the same integral interest. I feel it truly saved me from an other-wise solitary and quite possibly monastic life…"

"I am the product of endless books."
C. S. Lewis

Chapter Eight

"…Counting the beats.

Counting the slow heart beats.

The bleeding to death of time in slow heart beats,

Wakeful they lie…"

Counting the Beats, Robert Graves

After

Ed walked into the front room. The sunbeams through the open curtains fell softly all around, touching everything with a captivating dust. His eyes immediately drew to the outline of her exquisite body. How she draped herself without care or over thought, across the velvet chaise longue, as if exhausted. Not from lack of sleep he initially presumed, as he knew she was in bed more than she wasn't, or perhaps it was not a decent sleep she managed, thus leaving her in a permanent state of half-awake, half-dream. Either way he didn't know because she didn't tell him. She didn't tell him anything at all.

He stayed there at the doorway just looking at her, staring at the woman he loved, wondering if he watched her long enough he might be able to gain some clue, a reveal; some subtle key that would enable him to open her up again and rescue the women he remembered hidden inside. He waited. His heart was steady and his breathing quiet so as not to disturb, but his eyes remained keen and focussed. He did not know if she had even heard him come in.

Ed now looked onto the small coffee table, the biographies he had left for her, ones she had expressed an interest in when they had taken a lunch out together months ago, *before*, sat untouched with a soft downy film on them. Beside them was the large handmade bowl that they had chosen together when they were first married. That serene day down Clarenden Street, walking arm in arm, when Izzy noticed it propped up in the window of a very fine homeware shop. She had stopped for a long while outside and looked through the window at it in admiration. It was a wide, rough clay bowl, hand sculpted as a few of the artist's fingerprints were still visible on and around it. The inside had been filled with a cool, glossy dark grey glaze that carelessly, imperfectly spilt over and down the grainy edges outside. Within the shop there were little spotlights on the plinth that shone at it making it seem a piece of such ethereal beauty, as good as any ceramic that they had spent hours admiring in the Ashmolean and Pitt Rivers museums.

She was so enraptured when they purchased it from the cold efficient shop seller, that she giggled all the way home like a giddy infant. And Ed felt his chest expand and his head rise slightly higher, on the walk back, with the pride and glory of making her so happy, washing over him repeatedly with each peal of her joy.

This same bowl he looked at now had three large cracks running through it, breaking up the grey varnish like diverging rivers on an old map. Impossible to repair completely, though Ed had tried his best with his scratched clumsy fingers and the maddening tube of left-over super glue. The only adhesive they had in the house was that old, gold-coloured one left over from a Christmas project Izzy mastered the previous year, but it did the job. Forever broken as an unforgiving reminder of her physical rage that day back from the hospital; the screaming and the banging and the throwing about of precious things.

At the time Ed had spent all of his efforts to hold her back, to calm her and shush her quiet. To try and help her stop exploding as her fierce maternal hormones and her life-shattering grief overwhelmed her in a way she didn't know how to contain. How within the manic outbursts of cursing and pleading, the volume of pain that soaked into and amplified each of her words, she was alive, vivid and fighting. How he was transfixed at her physical movements of grabbing cushions and blankets, scratching and ripping into baby magazines and the few toys collected in their hopeful moments, the way her hips swayed and her arms contorted with energy burning from the feral anger and dark loss fire pit that roared within her. The unfairness of it all in that night, justified a whole frenzied dance of destruction to all the things that reminded her of a future they had planned for and what had been left behind in that ward.

But in looking at her, his Izzy, in watching the shape of her now solemn and silent as if already gone from this world, how he wished for, how he prayed for that emotional torrent to reappear. For Izzy to care enough to get up and do anything; one thing that would confirm to him, even in a small way that she was here willingly with him again.

A tiny shard of light reflecting off something smooth within the bowl caught Ed's eye as he walked towards it and peered in. It was the two small commas of Izzy's hearing aids, abandoned there together like twin little plastic foetuses. An explanation he concluded, of why Izzy hadn't registered his arrival. Although somewhere deep down, in a place Ed tried to ignore, perhaps in the voice of Carron, was the thought that even if she had heard the front door open and shut, she would still be lying there, without welcome or effort. Not turning to greet him with affection or enquiry but remaining motionless, far away from him like hiding behind the dimension of Lewis' invisible blanket.

Yet still, as the good British husband that he was, he walked over to Izzy and her stationary form, and kissed the top of her head softly. It was the gentle balance of not wanting to startle her now he knew she couldn't hear him approach, yet also to project somehow the genuine authenticity of his love for her in that singular, habitual gesture. He hovered there a few more moments unsure of what else to do. Her face was angled from him so he couldn't be certain if she was even awake as the window's reflection offered nothing more than a smear.

After a while he walked quietly into the kitchen to start something for them to eat, annoyed at his naivety for expecting anything more. The internal disappointment stung as he tried to switch his mind onto more trivial matters about food, yet the hum of helplessness and lack of intimacy lingered on. He stayed on in the comfort of the kitchen busy and unaware.

Unaware she had known he was home from the very second he returned. Unaware she had sharply felt his marital apprehension and solemn sadness, heavy and brooding, from all the way across the room. Unaware that when he had kissed her hair, it had caused the hot tears that were hiding inside her, to awaken and trickle silently down her cold cheeks as her hands strained to reach for him but could not move through the hard marble shell of her grief that encased her like a frightened insect trapped in carbon.

Ed put on the old radio to disturb the silence that was deafening him. The solitary bow and strings of Jacqueline du Pre performing Cello Suite No. 2 began filling the house, creeping through each room like radiator heat.

And the invisible glass bird swayed along, above the void, distant and beautiful, in time to cellist moves.

> "Stop all the clocks, cut off the telephone,
> Prevent the dog from barking with a juicy bone,
> Silence the piano and with muffled drum,
> Bring out the coffin, let the mourners come…"
>
> *Funeral Blues,* W. H. Auden

Chapter Nine

> "You can't go back and change the beginning,
> but you can start where you are and change the ending."
>
> C.S. Lewis

Before

June 14th 1997

Bannisters Bookshop
15 Little Clarendon Street
Oxford
OX8 7ER

Dear Mr Williams,

My name is Izzy Bannister and I am writing to invite you to attend a new and exciting project that we are getting up and running here in Oxford. We have formed a committee with fellow book store owners, local Authors, Illustrators, Publishing Houses, college Lecturers and my own self, with the plan to create a Festival dedicated to all things Books.

I have spoken to the University and they are making some beautiful lecture rooms available to us for our paying guests. The larger bookshops are sponsoring the advertisements on radio and local press and our fantastic publishing establishments are putting forward some of their more celebrated authors to give talks on a variety of subjects and genres. I believe so far these include fiction writers from young adults and older, Travel, Biographers, Mystery, Crime, Romance, Cookery and Poetry.

We would welcome the opportunity for you to become a part of this literary event. I understand you are already familiar with our esteemed city having studied here yourself at Corpus Christi College some years ago. In fact it is your fellow student, Marcia Daly, who as you may know runs the Lewis Carrol lectures at the Pitt Rivers Museum, suggested I try and contact to you. She felt this could be of interest knowing how hard you work to promote reading and learning, always striving for this essential pastime to reach wider audiences.

The Festival is penned in for the Saturday 4th of October as an initial trial. We will wait to determine from the customer attendance and reaction whether it will be successful enough to continue for the following year. As you know Oxford has a wealth of history in both the education of and the production of novels from centuries ago and carries on to this day, and we very much hope to raise awareness and inspire a passion and fevered interest in helping this continue to many more people than the normal tourism allows.

We were hoping you could join us for our preview Friday evening drinks at the Randolph on October 3rd, where we can gather all of the committee members, performers and pro ducers, to a vivacious night of creativity and conversations that can benefit all of us working in this wonderful industry.

All going well we will be starting something with a great future ahead, perhaps not just in our perfect Oxford, but in many other cities across the country, wouldn't that be a marvellous achievement.

I enclose a copy of The Unconsoled by Kazuo Ishiguro which I have recently discovered and very much enjoyed. Please feel free to acknowledge this as the very unashamed bribe it so obviously is, with the very clear intention of gaining your support and attendance.

Thank you very much for your time in reading this letter. I of course do appreciate how busy a man of your position must be. We do so hope you will be able to join.

With kind regards,

Isobel Bannister

As an established Agent in a well-known Publishing House, Ed received a great deal of post. That particular day his assistant Paul and business partner Carron were attending an auction on the new wave of American Author biographies due to be released. Customarily it was Paul's job to go through each handwritten letter, unsolicited manuscripts and printed correspondence and sort into piles of priority. There were important high-powered mail usually from established and respected colleagues in the publishing industry or business world, he believed appropriate for Ed's consideration, next were items of semi-importance which he would put on Carron's desk as she responded as Ed's first filter to potential new projects and book ideas. Finally, and most of them, were what Paul himself would handle which was the everyday requests of favours, school author signings pleas, autographs to excited fans or questions about specific novel incites by astute and obsessive readers.

This precise Friday Ed thanked Billy, the elderly postman who was doing the office rounds in the large London building where Fallon House were based, and took the large armful of packages and the like, wrapped with very strong elastic band securing them all together, united in their shared address, and placed them carefully down on his antique walnut desk.

The previous day he had hosted one of his newly formed Wilde lunches at Claridges with the latest, youthful Booker prize winner, an erudite illustrator of political cartoons as well as a very humorous Eastern European novelist hotly picked to be on the shortlist for the next Nobel Literature Prize. The meal was, as hoped, a huge success, with each invitee being great conversationalists on their own selves and subject as well as genuinely enjoying the wisdom and talent of those beside them. Ed directed this meeting as elegantly as a classical conductor, invisibly shaping and steering the flow to its most valuable peaks. It finished many hours later than his normal seven o'clock end, and he found himself so exhausted he booked a hotel room in one of the many handsome suites above the restaurant, to save him having to travel the twenty minute journey home.

He was grateful the office was quiet today The exuberance and delight of the night before meant he was capable of much less efficiency than normal and he was glad there were no witnesses close by to enjoy this rare bout of professional tardiness.

With the very welcomed hot coffee cup having warmed his big, capable hands, Ed cut through the straining elastic band with his desk scissors and slowly and methodically, went through the pristine paper mountain of post. A job he very much enjoyed doing in his earlier career years.

Halfway through the postal mound he came across the weighty, elegant pale cream package with his name, title and work address written carefully in black fountain ink. One of the stamps used he recognised as the previous year's Post Office celebratory collection of female authors; Austen, Brontes, Woolf, Potter, etc. The sender had alongside normal stamps, chosen the Agatha Christie one; a smaller image of the portrait he knew so well, and this opened a wide smile to his lips as he vividly remembered the enormous joy he had in reading all of sixty plus novels as a young lad. Lined up in their various colourful spines, Ed could envision them now proudly stood together on his childhood bedroom shelf, a much-wished for present from his book-mad parents, who in turn were delighted to buy him any form of respected reading material.

Normally he would have placed it on Paul's pile to deal with, but as it was this day was already off its normal trajectory and either the lack of last night's sleep or yesterday's surplus intake of excellent Bordeaux, or probably due to the heady combination of both it meant Ed decided to open it and discover for himself the funny, kind and intelligent letter enclosed. One he never would usually have had the chance to see. On any other day, Paul would have replied to, as always instructed when requests arrive from unknown functions needing Ed's out of office time, a polite but perfunctory 'thank you but unable to attend'.

However on this morning feeling intrigued and impressed both by the letter writer's obvious courage and kindness as well as excellent choice of novel he would take home and read that night, Ed reached for a pristine sheet of 180mg sky-blue paper with his company and title details embossed in gold at the top. He took up the Sheaffer silver ink pen from its carved marble holder and began composing a reply, thanking the sender for the very much anticipated book as well as accepting her generous request to include him in her Oxford Book Festival evening.

Ed wasn't sure why this bolt from the usual made him feel as cheerful as it did but he tried to intermittently brush it off throughout the rest of the business day but to no avail. That knot of curious delight stayed firmly inside him so quiet and anonymous he eventually continued unaware as to how it first started, but there it did stay; thanks to their initial correspondence, that plucky invite.

And this, of course we now know, was how it first began.

"I belong here. This is the land I have been looking
for all my life, though I never knew it till now."
C. S. Lewis

Chapter Ten

"Grief fills the room up of my absent child,

Lies in his bead, walks up and down with me,

Puts in his pretty looks, repeats his words,

Remembers me of all his gracious parts,

Stuffs out his vacant garments with his forms;

The, I have reason to be fond of grief?

Fare you well: had you such a loss as I,

I could give better comfort than you do.

I will not keep this form upon my head,

When there is such disorder in my wit.

O Lord! My boy, my Arthur, my fair son!

My life, my joy, my food, my all the world!

My widow-comfort, and my sorrows' cure!"

King John, Act three, scene four, William Shakespeare

After

I feel like I'm losing her. Every step I try and take back into the real world it's like she is going further away, to a place I can't reach her and I panic to think she might disappear forever, all over again, if I go too far. This half-way dream isn't true, yet it feels safer than any place I know.

But it's not where you are. And I know you have been waiting, so long, so good to me. You have held on even though it must feel I am lost to you too, maybe not coming back. If I chose you does that mean I can't have her anymore? Must I have one without the other?

But deep down I know what I have of her isn't true. It does sustain me somehow. It offers me enough nourishment for me to remain acute but only just. I am aware enough in that space that there's no room for others. It is a very selfish place. It is isolating and private. Only possible for her and I. Her spirit is possessive.

I can't sleep, I can hardly breathe. It's as if she waits for me in the stillest of moments, stopping the clocks, cutting off those telephones; that peripheral part of life, out of the corners of eyes, where the undead can dwell. It's enormous, it's exhausting, this grief is obsessive and invasive and I'm trapped within in; buried alive in this dense, muffled limbo.

But as time goes on it becomes harder to come home to. It's as if actual life is the false one and this dream-like state of having a child again, in whatever form it takes, is the truthful one.

But where are you? It's like I am watching you through glass, here but unseen and I call you but you cannot hear me. I stay like a ghost in my own home, a spectral observer within my own marriage. Yet I love you, I love you, I love you. Each day I hope you could come through the glass but I now know you never can. It isn't allowed. There are very definite rules in this spiritual half-way house. And I worry even if you are permitted; we would both be in it, misplaced to the rest of the world and never able to return.

I'm sorry my darling, I truly am. I've travelled to a space away from you, which I never wanted to do but when they left, when I was little, before, before, I remember finding them this way too; this mythical escape into a momentary other world, the doorway, the wardrobe where things are alive again and I am safe. It's timeless and solitary. It's a version of home long forgotten or mislaid. I lived there once but they didn't let me stay. I had to say goodbye in the end and grow up without them.

In one way that was easier. I had met them, seen them, loved them, held them. We had memories and experiences I could rewind and recall like a private cinema screen. It *was an endless loop of personal times chosen only by me, to fit whichever comfort I required in that moment, always there.*

With our girl nothing is or ever was. We never knew the colour of her eyes or the age she would walk. What her favourite flavour would be or how she would fit on our bed in between us when we'd read her the night time stories you'd chose. The sound of her voice or even her first cry was never for our world.

After the accident years ago they used to call me the silent child but it was actually her who truly was.

The past can be measured in time, hours, months or years but the future is infinite, no one can know, count or confirm and this is its frailty and its glory, never seen but not yet seen. How do you miss what you never had? How do you forget what you never knew?

I'm still here my darling. I promise I am. I'm trying to find a way back to you somehow. I'm so sorry it's taking so long. I'm so very tired. I'm always so tired. I'm tired of being afraid. I'm tired of being alone again. But mostly I'm tired of saying 'Goodbye' to the people I love.

So.

Sorry.

Darling.   X

"Nothing that you have not given away will ever really be yours."

C. S. Lewis

Chapter Eleven

"Some day you will be old enough to start reading fairy tales again."

C. S. Lewis

After

Ed sat down as he always did, on the lounge sofa opposite his wife, her curled up facing away from him and towards the closed window. With the dinner and dishes cleaned up and put away it was time for him now to begin his late evening reading from the manuscripts he had packed from the office to take home. The full satchel felt its usual weighty self as he removed the five copies of stories, all printed clearly, double spaced, twelve size and Times New Roman font. Paul had hole-punched and loosely threaded string through each separate novel's left hand margin making the turning of pages easier. Nicer to hold.

This evening was quiet, as was now the new normal. He had long since forgotten those nights within this very room, of the vibrant company of others, the pleasant rabble of group conversations and tinkling of laughter or the background hum of a well-known Arts programme on TV. He was sometimes tempted to play the radio to keep himself company acoustically but he had no such urge to do so tonight. There were no symphonies, no melodies or lyrics, no sound he wished to hear more than the woman seated across from him; silent and missing. He sat still, saddened by his obvious ineffectualness, his evident inadequacy.

He looked around the sitting room he knew so well. The two large collaged pictures they had chosen together from the local Headington Gallery, hung grandly together. They were of huge sculptured shapes made from delicate tissue papers. Two pieces bought by two people who wished future years of looking at them. He doubted Izzy had even glanced at them in nearly a year.

Those bright ocular curves of hot pinks and pale blues interlocked creating a new oval of violet colour in the centre, or the fine wisps of vivid orange cut into waves that over lapped the Payne's grey circles making a dark stain on the edges where they met. They still caused a stir of joy in him. The great aesthetics which pleased his eye had a definite impact, a brightness, a lifting of his inner self. He knew Izzy loved them once. He used to watch her study them, her alert green eyes fascinated by the imperfect delicate material against the shocking white card behind it. How if she looked long enough she would say the shapes would start to move, like a slow dance of tiny fractals merging together, like those tiny particles of light you strain to see floating behind closed eye lids. Her pretty, dark features shone and sparkled with soulful glee at trying to discover new, minute colourful combinations those papers made, held tight behind the heavy glass.

Ed's memory of moments when his wife was so in love with life, with art and books, with him, seemed so far away sometimes he would question if they even occurred. He was not convinced he hadn't simply made it up because he wished it, wanted it so much to be.

But to him sat there in the quiet that blanketed them, he questioned whether knowing joy that happened before but now gone was better than if it had never happened at all. It was a point he had repeated throughout this past year specifically, more often than he ever had. He would return again to his master C.S. Lewis' words 'The pain I feel now is the happiness I had before. That's the deal.' but stuck in his own agony, Ed could never decide if this was more a comfort or distress.

Sighing deeply he ran his hands over his eyes and cheeks as if to rouse a new idea from somewhere, shake up a plan that he hadn't yet thought of. He was the Prince unable to rescue his Princess locked up in her impenetrable Tower. The glass slipper he found had lost its owner, seemingly forever. He couldn't fight through the brambles and thickets to get near the Castle to awaken his sleeping wife. Although as desperate as the situation felt, there remained a sure part of him that refused to give up on her. Not simply through loyalty of vows or duty but because when he looked at Izzy he saw the person who had changed his life for the greater, for as long as they had *before...*

He glanced over to the bookshelf beside him. Ever full with just a token of his favourite fiction novels, short stories, poetry collections and a few biographies. Ed stared admirably at the worn spines from repeated openings, the various shades and typography used, each different, every design proudly showing an originality for their own piece. His hand moved across them until he reached his secondary school copy of W. H. Auden. He pulled it out and examined it closely. The smell of brittle yellowing pages pencilled on with his youthful comments and serious underlining of purposeful points. Scrawled observations like 'resonating', 'frustrated', 'indignant' and 'devoted' were dotted along every page like a random dictionary adjective game. Ed felt the warmth of juvenile innocence, a contentment and assuredness that had too long been absent in his recent self. Yet rather than depress him further it actually served as a vibrant reminder of how good and pure things once were and the taste of this clarity, spurred him on to do something, they would later look at as remarkable.

Ed sat back down on his chosen sofa spot with the Auden book, an old 'faber and faber' edition edited by Edward Mendelson, for once ignoring the pile of unread manuscripts on the table in front of him. The book's deep red printed background with the familiar 'ff' repeated all around was now a tired hue of two pale purples. The Susan Linney line drawn portrait of Wysten's crumpled and furrowed elderly face looked back at him with such sympathetic and kind eyes it felt he knew his own sorrows.

Ed searched the index for the poem he would feel most appropriate to begin with. Finding such one he opened out the book widely in his strong and capable hands, and began reading. Not his usual manner of viewing the written words only to himself, holding all the newly learnt pieces on his own, inside. No, this was not a solitary gesture. What Ed was starting, as of this moment, was a very deliberate shared event. A nightly habit he would establish in the pursuit of climbing that soaring Tower, finding that perfect shaped foot, clearing his pathway to the imprisoned Castle.

On page sixty-three, poem thirty-nine titled 'Oxford' Ed slowly and assuredly read out loud, pronouncing each careful line in the direction of Izzy, this entire nine verse poem. He enunciated each word and spoke with appropriate rhythm and emphasis as the description went along. Surprising himself at how poignant hearing sounds from husband to wife were again, elevated from the mundanity of daily errands and responsibilities. This was something outside of obligation. This was pure and heartfelt just by the very beauty of it. When he reached those penultimate stanzas his voice wavered, such was the poem's authentic effect, and he began to cry. For once in recent times it was not from the mourning of loss and grief but from the relief of finally offering something that could hopefully, pleadingly, connect him to his Izzy again.

At last he was using words that didn't come from him but through him; Words, both their very first loves. He worked with them every single day, bought them, produced them, and had endless hope and absolute faith in them. '*Words can save your life*', he remembered far down below from inside him somewhere. Maybe, maybe, maybe.

The glass bird swayed invisibly above them, ever so slightly on the gentle lifts of air his voice was making across the room. It rocked peacefully as it listened dream-like to the marvellous ode below.

> "...Ah, if that thoughtless almost natural world
> Would snatch his sorrow to her loving sensual heart!
> But he is Eros and must hate what must he loves;

And she is of Nature; Nature

Can only love herself.

And over the talkative city like any other

Weep the non-attached angels. Here too the knowledge of death

Is a consuming love: And the natural heart refuses

The low unflattering voice

That rests not till it finds a hearing.

Oxford, W. H. Auden.

Chapter Twelve

"You've a place in my heart no one else could have."

C. S. Lewis

After

Lying in the sitting room, waiting aimlessly for those few hours whilst Ed did his work until they would retire to bed was what Izzy was effortlessly used to; it was the comfort of the new normal. Not that Ed ever knew it, but Izzy felt more settled when he came home.

The daily isolation made time pause into endless periods, hours encapsulating all seasons, any weather, every time of day, holding her possessively tight within it. All that alone, daylight time was made useful by her. Izzy closed her mind down, and trained herself to find a serene space. She had mastered how to create a mental clarity and be able to dream of a place with their daughter living in it. She was trapped in this dwelling, fuelled by a mother's imagination so strong, its will volcanically charged with emotional desperation, the utter anguish of a once pregnant woman who returned home with empty arms.

In this abstract visualisation, the child's age would change from a newly born baby, to a toddler, up to the age of six at the very most. She was a lovely fair skinned, pale blonde haired little girl with wide green eyes that would stare back at Izzy, directly into a place she had never felt before. A small corner hidden in the upper left part of her heart chamber was where this look would settle, filling Izzy up with such an unmatchable maternal satisfaction that nothing else, in all of heaven and earth to her, seemed to matter.

Some days she would be brushing her daughter's long hair, fashioning it into high pony tails or complicated braids, using small silver clips formed like tiny, metallic insects. Others Izzy would be feeding her swaddled baby, freshly bathed, as it suckled happily onto her plump lactating breast, staring up at her mother with innocent adoration.

Some of Izzy's favourite visions were of her beautiful girl, sat upon her knee as she tried to speak new words Izzy had been teaching her. The new shapes her small, perfect mouth made, her little brow furrowed sweetly in concentration, her excited eyes as she managed to pronounce 'Hi' or 'Ta' or 'Dada'.

The low thud of the front door when Ed arrived home, made their daughter suddenly tuck herself quickly down into Izzy's neck fold, between her shoulder and the top of her arm, feeling like a warm breath, shapeless, invisible but emphatically spiritually present. Izzy froze, laying there in the hope she could hold on to her, that she wouldn't go away too soon, that their daughter would wait long enough, till his welcome kiss on Izzy's head which she would in turn passed downwards in the hope their ghost-child could feel it's touch. For a small second in time and space the three existed together again; a crossover of worlds, so fragile in its actuality that the merest blink could extinguish it. One impossible but flawless moment that gave Izzy such a surge of love for them both she felt blissfully complete, whole, in this achievement of their formerly broken family.

And as quick as this fantasy had been created, Izzy sensed it was gone again. Off away to a place she was unable to visit at night times. The presence of Ed now formed a certain stubborn reality that was unshakeable. His movements on rote, from stairs to longue to kitchen to bathroom instilled a firm resolution of the actual. It produced an area where imagination and wishful calling fell away like water draining from an unplugged sink. Swirling and folding down in to an unknown darkness, its use spent and the user grateful for its service.

As much as Ed was inadvertently the plug-puller of these dreams, this also meant he was the reason for Izzy to return to a form of sanity, and she was at most times relieved for this disturbance. Despite her love, it bothered her how all-consuming the mother-daughter periods were becoming, how it was starting to feel more real than Ed's one she would return to.

She was scared that if she explained to Ed this fantastical place she was daily living in, told him the way she had found a secret parental home, he would never understand, not believe her, think her mad. He had in their beginning, fallen in love for her sharp, intelligent mind and she worried that he could never understand, or worse, pour away all his love for her, as she wasn't the wife she had shown such promise to be.

How could she bare to lose them both? How could she ever keep them both? Izzy was afraid of it all. She was frightened of it, that it would stay longer and grow bigger until there was no room for anything else, till it was enormous, until it one day wouldn't run and hide away at the sound of the front door.

"It is hard to have patience with people who say, 'There's no death' and 'Death doesn't matter'.
There is death. And whatever is matters. And whatever happens has consequences,
and it and they are irrevocable and irreversible.
You might as well say that birth doesn't matter."

A Grief Observed, C. S. Lewis

Chapter Thirteen

"I fell in love with her courage, her sincerity and her flaming self respect. And it's these things I'd believe in, even if the whole world in wild suspicions that she wasn't all she should be. I love her and that is the beginning and end of everything."

F. Scott Fitzgerald

Before

A noise can be an actual, physical thing. Sound of any description creates specific energy across the atmosphere, touching or changing another, sometimes with only the slightest of perception. To someone with the hearing condition such as Izzy's, they are able to detect a wealth of information to surrounding circumstances, if having trained themselves acutely enough. Internal silence brings a clear white canvas on which even the tiniest drops of aural colour appear sharp and vivid. Opening and closing a door, leaves a slight punch in the air, the cooler breath from letting the outside breeze in is secondary as the dull wooden thud shifts miniscule dust particles off a cold coffee cup, another room away, all observed by the deaf listener. The slight whoosh of a vowel being beautifully pronounced forms a pop in the air stream that brushes upon those invisible hairs ever-risen on high cheek bones. Each vowel a different facial stroke to another until a whole alphabet of bubbles touches the skin like a corporeal code.

"She always hated her hearing aids." Uncle Alexander confessed to Ed, one time at a birthday dinner Izzy had prepared for him. "She would take them out and leave them in various secret, hidden corners of the flat like a stubborn spy. Always with the same excuse of, 'But I don't need to hear to read,' of which she was of course always doing, to which I would then have to counter, 'but you do need them to listen out for the bloody doorbell my darling!'" Alexander chortled. His round face and heavy set neck jingled merrily over his starched white shirt collar. His colourful silk bowtie, ever expertly tied, sat neatly within it. He looked the very essence of a quaint English scholar. He certainly had the brain for an Oxford one but Ed often wondered, without the loyal pull of the family bookshop always moored to him, what he could have become in an alternative career.

"Did she always need to wear them?" Ed enquired as he stood close to Alexander but moved his eyes away to look over at his incredible wife; her hands busy redressing the table flowers, her face happy as the twist of a smile formed on her lips as she listened to Marcel beside her, reminiscing about his recent travels to Peru.

"Well from nine years old, you know, since the accident. She was an elective mute for a while too." Ed turned sharply back round, his eyes widened with surprise at this information. Izzy was wonderful at so many things but talking him through the tragedies of her past was certainly not one of them. Ed never pressed her for more, she seemed pleased to not have to think about those darker years especially now her life had taken such an unexpected but very grateful, fortunate turn.

"Yes I believe it had everything to do with the horror of losing my brother and his wife, naturally there would have to be some painful effects for any child so young to deal with. Her bodily injuries from the car accident, ears aside, were relatively minor, but it was never the physical wounds we were worried about. It's always the emotional ones that go so much deeper, don't you think?" Ed murmured and nodded his head in agreement as he leant forward slightly, reaching for the open bottle of Merlot, pouring more into Alexander's drained glass, welcoming him to continue.

"Two years we lost her for. Not a thing we could do. Marcel was marvellous with his patience and care for her. He taught her words in sign language which I disagreed with as I thought it was indulging her enforced distance and would extend her not returning to the real, speaking world but god damn it he was right. Over time and with the right selection of novels we would carefully put on the side table of her bed, she began to come out of wherever it was she'd been, and started to talk again. It was a huge relief I can tell you."

They both took a moment to look over at Izzy and Marcel laughing together across the room. His gentle, wide brown hands lifting her own as he twirled her around in the style of the South American dance move he had been so vibrantly describing. She looked relaxed and delighted to be demonstrated such an exultant tale. Her brown wavy hair swishing on her slight shoulders and her jade green eyes shone, sparkling with the pleasure of being surrounded by her most favourite people in one room, for such a celebratory occasion.

The soft Cello music playing on the speaker in the background trickled slowly and willingly into each of them. The notes playing gently rocking those happy four in that warm spring room, into a loving lull.

And life was good.

Life was very good.

For now.

You see, I want a lot.
Maybe I want it all;
the darkness of each endless fall,
the shimmering light of each ascent.

So many are alive who don't seem to care.
Casual, easy, they move in the world
as though untouched.

But you take pleasure in the faces

of those you know they thirst.

You cherish those

who grip you for survival.

You are not dead yet, it's not too late

to open your depths by plunging into them

and drink in the life

that reveals itself quietly there,

Rainer Maria Rilke

Chapter Fourteen

"If I knew words enough, I could write the longest
love letter in the world and never get tired."
F. Scott Fitzgerald

After

The gentle buzz that danced over Izzy's eardrums and cheeks like tiny, familiar fireworks

shocked her into attention. She almost gasped out in surprise it had been so long since any

aspect of their evening routine had changed. It was many months since Ed had tried to talk,

to speak out loud towards her. The two plastic commas of hearing aids remained

obstinately safe in their grey bowl home, untouched save for the small covering of dust that

had settled over them as time went on. The dish Ed looked in religiously each homeward

return, to confirm if Izzy was still gone to him; their cracked bowl.

Looking through the window to see Ed's reflection there felt safer than turning

around to face him in actuality. Somehow watching him with that glass between their eye

contact meant she was there but also not. It felt that this was the true-ist reflection; this ever

present distance; that continuing cage.

But for the first time in so very long she looked up to see Ed's mouth wide open and

speaking. At first she wasn't sure if she had seen it correctly or simply another version of

her imagination taking over. A few moments to study and check, peering more

purposefully at his image whilst his eyes were cast downward, reading the lines off the

page, Izzy confirmed that he was indeed talking out loud. Gentle curves of air brush passed

her shoulders carrying a warmth of wind that was previously not there. Tiny splatters of dots, like atoms, tickle her neck as they have been expelled out towards her and now bounce back from the closed window touching her face like a memory.

The energy in the whole room had shifted. She stares astounded at this new event. Her huge green eyes wide and curious, her pulse leaping and bounding as Ed continues, his mouth rounded and animated, his brow furrowed with care.

The breezes between them are rolling and curling across the room as invisible missives, gestures from each pronounced word to another. Izzy can see the book he is reading from but unsure of which poem he is speaking. There are so many she can recall, so many that mean so much to her, to him, to them both.

She tries to guess from the lifts and putts in the draft which shapes mean what. Her brain becomes busy with trying to translate, using both the contoured air and the moving forms of his lips to identify this message but everything feels maddeningly sluggish, it has been so long since she has pushed herself to do anything outside of her head.

As she watches Ed complete those final lines, noticing how his shoulder move almost unperceptively lower, his lips slowing down to acknowledge the ending of this wondrous verse through the reflection. She gazes at his soft, sad face responding with such a genuine, heart felt reaction that Auden's words had affected. Ed's initial bravery seeping silently away from his throat as the poem ends, Izzy notices the tears fall quietly from his eyes and her heart breaks for him in a new way than it was ever broken before.

Fury begins to surge within her, burning along each vein from her feet to her scalp; she feels the fire from her helplessness scorching her insides like a punishment: Pain as if a true physical reality.

"I love you, I love you, I love you!!!!" she screams at him ferociously and urgently, but it will not come out of her lungs. "I'm sorry, I love you, I'm so sorry!!!" she shouts as violently as she knows how in the direction of the window, to that almost-view of her beautiful husband, but nothing escapes from her. All hope and joy and gratitude and comfort stay trapped firm, bound tight inside her solid body, the heat from it all turning her pale bones to ash.

Exhausted and frightened, Izzy stops trying to talk and just lies there, alone on the chair, silent and powerless. She watches Ed in his strong, elegant handwriting, write the poem down on a piece of their correspondence paper and place it in the bowl for her to see later. "If she ever wanted", he thought, "if she even cares." The haunting quote from her Uncle looped round in his head, 'I don't need the hearing aids to read…' and Ed didn't know if that was a help or a hindrance to this new task.

Ed walked out of the room trying to remember why he started this act. His self, taking this time to believe again in something he once took great faith in. He sighed out trying to gain some sort of inner strength from those poetic phrases he had just absorbed. 'It would take time', he thought, 'the great things always do', he reassured.

And what of that lost bird, over that huge scary abyss? The one they could not see. The one who always watched: The one that had been swinging to the new shapes in the air.

"It's a funny thing coming home. Nothing changes. Everything looks the same, feels the same, even smells the same. You realise what's changed is you."

F. Scott Fitzgerald

Chapter Fifteen

After

Carron sat at her large oak desk. Piles of manuscripts to both the left and right of her were stacked in neat rows, coloured paper stickers were threaded throughout the pages indicating where she had made comments or crossings in her infamous red pen. The laptop in front of her showed forty-eight emails unread. Most of these were concerned enquiries on behalf of nervous authors, a few were from her American and European counterparts confirming details of overseas contracts she had expertly constructed and a final one was from Hank McGregory, owner of a huge Publishing House in Edinburgh, proposing a very lucrative job offer if she ever wanted to leave Ed and Paul, 'her boys', at Fallon House.

Such offers came relatively regularly to Carron being as well thought of and admired in the industry that she was, but as ever she stared at the screen with a whisper of a smile and left it unread. She could let him down nicely with kind but brief reply later. Hank had been emailing her such offers on a monthly basis since she met him three years ago at the Man Booker Prize evening. Remembering his Scottish charm over shared whiskies at the bar, had he really looked attractive in the roguish outdoorsy way? She queried. He was built broad but definitely trim due to all of his sporting outside pursuits he was telling her about. There was nothing different in their ages she guessed to be of note, and could see no wedding band, but she had held herself back from completely opening up to him with stories of her own life and interest. Not that she was convinced he was after anything more than to professionally help him build up the business of publishing she knew so well, but something about his jovial messages he wrote before attaching his hopeful contract felt playful in a respectful way, and on her lonelier occasions she did feel tempted to sometimes respond perhaps a little more personal than before.

"Sorry to disturb you Carron but I was going to head off now. Paul has left early for his conference in Bristol, so are you happy to lock up or do you want to finish up too?"

The warm, treacly voice of Ed reached her ears like a blessing and her lips opened involuntary into a wide smile as she looked towards him, his head poking out from her open doorway. His words suggested he was ending the work day but by the weight of his brown leather satchel hanging off the shoulder, a present she had given him they day he made her Partner, she knew he would have hours of reading still left to do tonight. A wave of annoyance rose over her as she thought of him so busy and dedicated to this work they shared yet knowing he would be going home to even more effort, tending to Izzy and her fragility and tragedy.

Ed never remarked or complained but Carron could all too easily imagine their home life, Izzy drowning in her self-induced melancholy and absorbing depression, whilst Ed would use all his energy to tidy up their home, make decent food for them both to eat, worrying she needed to keep her strength up, exhausting himself with her practical care even though it was never reciprocated. His own decency masking the lack of love and support he neither demanded nor expected anymore, but Carron believed he so justifiably deserved.

Carron had always been short tempered and dismissive of those females who got by in life with no talents or hard work to excel them. Their simpering wiles and gentile faked manners smacked of life laziness and feminine manipulation abhorrent to her hard earned and defiant feminist views. Not that her initial opinion of Izzy was such. She had at first admired her joint running of the family book shop as well as he many organisational skills to promote Fallon House's new authors or celebrate publications though hosting numerous dinners, book signings or parties to include a mixture of professionals. That seemed a world away now, ever since, since…that unfortunate incident, but it was almost a year now and things had not improved, in fact Carron believed things had got distinctly worse and felt she couldn't hold it back any longer. Was she not Ed's friend as well as colleague? She asked herself. Was it not her duty, her moral responsibility to give him a clear perspective and well-intended advice during such difficult times when he was too close to it all? Too unsure?

"Actually Ed, do you have a minute?" Carron asked and her tone was as such that only a positive affirmation for this suggestion would do.

Getting up, Carron walked over to the smaller drinks table in the corner of her office, next to the two comfortable leather armchairs that were strategically positioned by the warm heater on the adjoining wall, and upturned two crystal glasses. This designated area was where she charmed clients to join their, recruited literary editors to work alongside them and amusedly listened to publishing creatives describing their exciting plans to promote the latest author that was under Fallon protection. It was a successful space, cleverly designed to exude confession and trust.

She had hung a framed painting of Uccello's The Hunt in the Forest, an oil painting she had very much enjoyed seeing time and time again in her father's old Art History tomes he would regularly read, making notes on for his classes. It was an important piece to her to look at and study in those quieter office moments. Certain work days, aware of the parallels of from her office to the canvas, she was not sure exactly of whether she was the hunter or the hunted but what she was always sure of was that she so very much enjoyed being part of the sport.

Ed looked at his watch, his brow furrowed in concern. It read 17.33. He knew that Izzy would be at home, that was a given. He knew she would be lying in her front room seat, quiet and somewhere far away. In returning home by six o'clock, he would get in a produce a meal for them to share by seven, separately in the end, but made for them initially, together. Would she notice if he was late? Would she mind that he gave her the food at eight? Half past? At all?

What he didn't want to think about, what he never wanted tested and have confirmed was if he wasn't there, if he never came home, if the meals would end and the front door never open, would she care? Would she feel relieved? Would she even notice?

Unaware of the private monologue that was going through Ed's mind at that precise moment, Carron confidently poured two large glasses of the amber, smoky, single malt that she knew Ed enjoyed. A gift sent from a very happy and generous Illustrator client a few weeks previous.

Perhaps it was the gentle authority Carron projected over him at that moment. The deep relief of someone else, a trusted adult to take over a decision, however small, and show him what would be good for him to do for a while. Unburden him from his own choices or concerns. A small gesture of personal kindness he had felt so powerlessly deprived of in recent months; understandable perhaps, but still wanting.

The brown leather satchel he had been holding now felt heavy and cumbersome, as if it was filled with bricks rather than books. Removing it from his shoulder and placing it carefully on the floor beside him felt joyful, an unexpected sweet release. As he smiled and walked over to one of Carron's weathered but comfortable armchairs.

He was unaware at first that the shedding of his bag was not the only thing to be divested that evening.

"It's not the load that breaks you down. It's the way you carry it."

C. S. Lewis

Chapter Sixteen

"Go try and save a soul, and you will see how well it is worth saving, how capable it is of the most complete salvation. Not by pondering about it, nor by talking of it, but by saving it, you learn its preciousness."

Phillip Brooks

After

"I'm glad Richard Solomon has started to write again. It has been quite a while now and his fans were getting so impatient for a follow up. Book number four in that genre particularly, after the first three received so well, sometimes causes a crash in confidence. That spark of initial energy and inspiration that can seemingly flow so fully before the crushing doubt creeps in, paralysing the writer to feel unable to continue." Ed sighed. He had seen it happen often over the years. Amongst Publishers and Agents it was titled the 'Terrifying Trinity' of Crime. "I now however, have his full manuscript with me tonight to read through. I'll let you know if he keeps in that glamourous Romanian side-kick you liked so much."

He spoke up to the air between them. He talked to that obscured reflection of her in the window, like a smudged portrait in charcoal. There was not enough clarity of vision to confirm she had lifted her eyes to him through it. Ed still continued to speak. He had a strength of hope tonight that had been growing since his evening poetry readings began. He felt a sense of optimism to make a dent in the quiet that pulled down invisibly between them like a heavy curtain.

"Richard is a nice man, very upbeat and jolly. He has a wonderful laugh, like that Opera singer we spent an afternoon with at Abi's wedding: Full bellied and infectious."

Settling himself down on the couch, pre-novel scripts piled on the left corner of the table, glass of red wine in the centre and pens and pencil, and a blank white sheet of paper lined up at the ready, Ed reached in his bag for the new volume of work he purchased in his lunch break earlier that day.

He had, unusually for him, left his desk for the allotted twelve till one o'clock slot and walked six streets away on the busier high street where the main shops began. The large Wallow and Hibberd bookshop was placed between a Cancer charity centre and a high end shoe store, and inside it was pleasingly full.

A vast selection of society milled and wondered about the shelves. Both students and teachers browsed through the curriculum texts and their criticisms; mothers and toddlers reached towards brightly coloured picture books and soft toy displays; men from elderly to teens looked at the new paperback fictions coming in; seemingly unemployed twenty-somethings dotted around the self-help and travel; a disabled wheelchair user rifled through the plastic bagged piles of Anime. All this activity, this hub of learning and discovering filled Ed with a burn of pride from his feet to his scalp, books and all their families thereof, were important; definitely, essentially, happily important.

He took himself to the far back row of shelves, along the wall in between Biography and Photography. Hidden away in its darkened corner space a narrow, soft velvet armchair sat there as if abandoned but surely placed purposely by another, fellow enthusiast. Ed's large hand gently ran over the spines of the middle book shelf, slowly and softly: So many names so familiar to him. He smiled when he came across the ones printed from his own Fallon Publishing: A few he remembered seeing on his desk years ago waiting for consideration, written by the Poet's own original and inimitable hand.

It was always an honour, he thought, a privilege to be asked to see someone's draft of their work. The invitation to view such intimate thoughts, the most private expressions and considerations or the vulnerable writings of a person who took time out of their life to stop, give themselves permission to invest days, months or more, to write something they felt worth recounting. To Ed they were courageous.

However, he also knew that the bravery with which they started rarely remained by the time they had completed; and completing really was for the very few. He often recalled Hemingway's quote about the hardest part about writing is finishing it and he did believe this absolutely. Like Ed's favourite Auden, the difference between a professional and an amateur was usually both the self-belief and self-control. Writing required work, even if the mood did not take you or the muse was lacking. Wysten Auden would get up each day and compose with an almost monastic discipline. He, like many successful others, took charge of his talent and made it his job by it being a job. Poems, Novels, Plays, stories did not just happen, they were made as assuredly and deliberately as a carpenter constructs his cabinet or a mason builds a wall.

The Poetry section of this particular Wallow and Hibberd was extensive and impressive. It catered for both the classic and established Poets as well as the more modern or obscure ones, including handmade or limited printed copies of newer works. The choice was joyful to Ed, being able to open up a physical version of these words, the weight and size of each edition, their letter press, their inked-scents, was intoxicating. It was the same sensation to him internally as some others might feel heart-full exuberance and sacred fervour, walking into a Church.

Today he looked at the edition nearing the middle of the alphabet order. One he was familiar with but not for many years. To be sure there would be the perfect one to read out later on, Ed cautiously prized the volume out of its space between the tightly filled tomes and sat himself on the plush and ever so comfortable chair. Crossing his legs, his right hand reaching into his top jacket pocket for the reading glasses he reluctantly depended on more and more, Ed settled into this sacrosanct moment and opened the handsome, pristine first page.

Hours later in their front room, Izzy lay on the chaise longue, silent. The blanket on her was more for comfort than warmth and her mind was quieter now, still yet alert like an ember. She realised she was waiting, that she was anticipating this part of the evening's new event. Izzy was, unable to help herself but looking forward to hearing what her husband had chosen for this night.

Henry Wadsworth Longfellow

The Day Is Done

The day is done, and the darkness
Falls from the wings of Night,
As a feather is wafted downward
From an eagle in his flight.

I see the lights of the village
Gleam through the rain and the mist,
And a feeling of sadness comes o'er me
That my soul cannot resist:

A feeling of sadness and longing
That is not akin to pain,
And it resembles sorrow only
As the mist resembles the rain.

Come, read to me some poem,

Some simple and heartfelt lay,

That shall soothe this restless feeling,

And banish the thoughts of day.

Not from the grand old masters,

Not from the bards sublime,

Whose distant footsteps echo

Through the corridors of Time.

For, like strains of martial music,

Their mighty thoughts suggest

Life's endless toil and endevor;

And to-night I long for rest.

Read from some humbler poet,

Whose songs gushed from his heart,

As showers from the clouds of summer,

Or tears from the eyelids start;

Who through long days of labor,

And nights devoid of ease,

Still heard in his soul the music

Of wonderful melodies.

Such songs have power to quiet

The restless pulse of care,

And come like the benediction

That follows after prayer.

Then read from the treasured volume

The poem of thy choice,

And lend to the rhyme of the poet

The beauty of thy voice.

And the night shall be filled with music,

And the cares, that infest the day,

Shall fold their tents, like the Arabs,

And as silently steal away.

Ed couldn't help but pause at the splendour of the piece, and again the act of speaking those lines aloud had an ever greater impact than his elated discovery of it within the compilation in the shop earlier. Those incredible statements ringing in his ear like peeling cathedral bells. He gave himself a moment, eyes closed to take in the concept of Longfellow's missive, the genius of his points. Ed sat with the hope those thoughtful words transposed themselves across the room to Izzy.

And that pale ever-watching bird above them wished so much it could carry that man's intentions over to the quiet lady. That it could sing that important message from its tiny beak, sharing all the hope that voice had contained: Tendering it over like a Dove's olive branch.

Please. Come. Back.

With his eyes shut Ed had no way of seeing Izzy's face, however muted that glass reflection was: To see her lips part and smile, to see her eyes wide and brighten. And his effort so clearly understood as if delivered direct from that invisible bird itself, made her marble-grief shell crack open just a fraction more, even wider than before, such were the power of those beautiful words.

As Ed lifted the pen to write the poem down for Izzy onto the good A4 paper in front of him, he felt a slight shift in the air: Nothing to be sure of. It was a fraction of an energy that moved with atom-size from distant indifference to the possible side of care: As invisible as a wish.

"The birds they sang

at the break of day

Start again

I heard them say

Don't dwell on what

has passed away

or what is yet to be

Ah the wars they will

be fought again

The holy dove

she will be caught again

Bought and sold

And bought again

The dove is never free

Ring the bells that can still ring

Forget your perfect offering

There's a crack in everything

That's how the light gets in"

Anthem, Leonard Cohen

Chapter Seventeen

"They slipped briskly into an intimacy from which they never fully recovered."
F. Scott Fitzgerald

Before

They lay naked and entwined. Izzy's pale, slender legs wrapped possessively around Ed's

muscular, ones, like two strong roots of solitary, ancient trees knotting together. Ed's chest,

puffed and sweaty, rose up and down gently as his breathing resumed to its normal pace.

Her pleasured gasping had since quelled and all that was left to be seen or heard from her

after their post-coital adventures was the slightly reddened cheeks that tellingly always

darkened when aroused. His kind, worldly grey eyes looked lovingly into hers as his smile

towards her made a repeated one on her own lips.

The many previous hours of sexual activity had both physically exhausted and

mentally excited them. They were now deep into hungered conversations.

"Do you know what I love?" Izzy said with a simple, open tone.

Ed crossed his brow and thought about how to answer this. One of the many things

he enjoyed about being in Izzy's company was he was never sure which direction her brain

would dash off in. She was so curious and questioning about things she saw or read, people

she watched but didn't understand; she wrapped these unknowns up into a tight ball of

wool inside her eager brain until she could work out the correct way to unravel it. Nothing

necessarily had to be hidden in its centre. The woollen ball would reveal no secret gem

squirreled away internally, it was the act of untangling the whole piece to its straightened

end that was the jewel itself. Answers, knowledge, understanding, these were the fuels that fed Izzy's hungry cerebral fires and as an observer or an included guest, as Ed often now was on these perceptual journeys, they were always a gorgeous time of discussion and discovery that tied them both together intimately and invisibly, unknown to others on the outside.

"What I love is…" taking his face into her small, soft hands and kissing him lightly on his lips. "The power words have to inspire a verbal intimacy, a personalisation for a couple that others are excluded from; that sort of privacy of language, beautifully and possessively belonging only to those chosen two.

Take for example when Uncle Alex met Marcel it was at Freud's Jazz Café, at an evening where single adult people went along to not only listen to that intoxicating and sensual live music but also with the hope of finding perhaps a similar other for company. When seeing Marcel coming off the stage from his piano playing, Alex was too shy to approach him immediately and no doubt after an excruciating amount of eye contact and lack of any practical motion, thankfully Marcel himself wondered over and began a conversation. 'Hey there.' Simple, direct, open: two words, neither pushy nor coy. Uncle Alex petrified with his very British anxiety and apprehension decides to simply smile and wave back. No words possible apparently, just a wave, I mean, poor thing. I can't imagine another man on this earth that knows more words in the English language than he does, he's obsessive about it, but on this occasion utterly speechless.

Luckily Marcel powers on, encouraged by this older man's sweet and panicked nature, and talks to him until Alex's voice repaired and operational once again and thankfully they haven't stopped talking together since.

Now I'm absolutely sure Alex wasn't presenting some sort of game plan, being distant and remote in order to reel in a potential mate. This was definitely a petrified reaction to possible actual romance and yet the end result is a victory. Body language certainly has a lot to do with this but also words, no words, other words or even worse the wrong words could have impacted that introduction irreparably and they would have missed out on their twenty-five years together.

'Hey there!' is two words. And to this day, two and a half decades later, they still share this joke between them. Every morning Marcel will wake up and start with 'Hey' then chose another word to follow it depending on the mood he's in or the attitude he reads on Alex's face. So something like, 'Hey Bear' when he's feeling attentive, 'Hey Beautiful' when he thinks Alex feels down, 'Hey Porcupine' is often said when a bitchy or mean comments has just been announced. Somehow the 'Hey' encases all of these seconds parts with love, somehow whatever the following noun or adjective happens to be depending on the circumstances, it's already been wrapped in the first part so it can never be too bad or not careful."

"That is amazing. I never knew that they did that. It's remarkable to think of them having a tradition all from that first welcome." Ed was genuinely touched by this long lasting ritual that recorded and reminded them of their ongoing love from its origins.

"However, on the other side of word number greetings hooking you in from the start," Ed recalled a similar conversation on opening lines he had had earlier this month when out for a work drink. "Paul from my office is convinced he can find a potential sexual partner for the evening with the same four words. Always the same, never needs to alter them as his success rate is so high. As a very intelligent young man he has spent years determining the very best way to use his Cambridge studies, centuries of Classical through to Modern Literature, embracing everything from Dante, Satre, Irving and Kundera and he believes he has amalgamated all this knowledge into four words to entice and embrace another, be it just for one night. Like a dissertation for the definitive sexual advance."

"Four words, well, that's endless with all Paul's impressive education and constant reading. Four words." Izzy mused, her brain calculating some of the infinite combinations of heart-wrenching testaments, snatches of breathlessly loving written lines. She floated from the 'heaven kiss' quote from Pasternak's Doctor Zhivago to Hodkin's The Evolution of Mara Dyer speech about 'being made mine each thousand lives', right until one of her favourite lines about 'if needing a life to come take it', from Chekov's The Seagull. All of these were far too long of course, she was so keen to know how on a literary beach where every grain of sand represented such hauntingly beautiful prose, could someone possibly whittle down a four line note, regularly used, unchanged and apparently almost flawless in its affect.

"Any clues?" her eyes widened with happiness the new precious discovery that she would soon know.

"Surprisingly not a classics quote, which might disappoint you I know, but more of a statement. A false one at that." Ed remarked, his mouth half-cocked in a smirk as he watched Izzy's eyelashes flutter with eagerness whilst her brain busied itself. Her teeth bit down on her lower lip reflecting her inner concentration.

"Umm, I just can't imagine, there's too many!" She laughed which in turn made Ed do the same. "Oh goodness, right…Count your lucky stars. Take me home now. Help I'm being kidnapped! Stop or I'll shoot?"

"None of the above, I'm afraid, although I actually am afraid at the aggressive moving towards quite frankly violent threats that are escalating with your guesses." His face displayed mock offensive, her smiled widened further.

"You have to imagine Paul on his night out, fashionably dressed. Clubs or Bars packed to bursting. Handsome young males all jostling for the best catch and then Paul comes slickly over delivering his impeccable line of… Hi, I'm Ron Weasley.'"

Izzy burst out laughing remembering Paul's ever-youthful pale, eager face and how his wild ginger locks that were normally smoothed down conventionally in the work situation, leapt free the moment the five thirty chimed as if they had an alarm clock all of their own. His striped scarf, which as she thought about it now, looked less College colours and more Gryffindor house, took altogether a new element of interpretation. She wasn't surprised if in his velvet, tailored jacket's inner pocket he carried a make-shift wand.

"You see, out and about amongst 'many taller, handsomer' – his words, or richer, using this introduction he believes it projects the correct amount boyish cocky charm and self-effacing humility, and from the results he attests to, it really works."

"Hhmmm, interesting…" Izzy conceded only slightly, her eyes slanting as if requiring an extra example of this deceptive male mini-words-strategy to convince her further.

"And even better…number wise, his friend Austin apparently only needs to use one, just one singular, perfect word to win over his potential mate." Ed said.

"Oooo now that is impressive. Without fail?" Izzy enquired, stroking his upper arm delicately with her fingers.

"No losers yet my secret source, that would be Paul, assures me. Works every time." Ed's eyes narrowed with feigned arrogance which made Izzy giggle happily into the warm space between them.

"So that one word would be…" she questioned as her lithe body quickly looped around so she was now straddling him, trapping him willingly underneath, her face serious with anticipation as she was waiting, animatedly, to hear this famous response.

Ed lay below her watching the morning sun filtering through the small crack in the old curtains bathing her form in its gold tones as if she was some kind of ethereal being. It took him a moment to gather himself back to their conversation, so entranced and distracted he was how perfect that moment felt to him.

"Wow," he spoke eventually, both answering the question and also with absolute genuine reaction to her there and then. "Wow," he repeated, his eyes stilled in the desperate effort of trying to photograph her with them, in those precious seconds of time, to somehow record this truthful image of her, so he could faultlessly recall it whenever he needed to remember, tonight, tomorrow, later, for as long as the years that he may have.

Izzy sighed pleasurably at hearing this solution. Yes, 'wow' made sense to her. Three little letters, one huge reaction. It meant the observer was impressed, that the watcher was showing great delight and captivation at that new, original person who had caught their eye. It was a beautiful use of the word as it suggested a dazzle-ment, an awe-struck response triggered by the person you wanted to sway towards you. Authentic or not, this would again be down to the body language projected at the time of its utterance, but the fact that those three little letters could cause such a regular response of gratitude and awakening, made her feel great waves of joy at such discovery.

"Wow," she whispered breathily into Ed's left ear as she leant across him, her thighs tightening his own steady beneath. And he moved his head to kiss her, purposefully and passionately. Their lips interlocking in parallel, then opening up so their tongues could continue the communication their speech had begun. Rising himself up he held her back firmly towards him, her uncovered breasts pushed against his solid chest that longed for her. His heartbeat was pumping quicker as he felt the hot blood rush around all inside him to the rhythm of that heavy beat; and the whooshing sound was replaced by the singular lyric, 'wow', 'wow', 'wow' as he continued to kiss her, falling helplessly in love with her with every beat of that sound.

After a minute Izzy pushed back a little and continued talking, but softer now, into his shoulders and over his cheeks. "I like the idea of an exact number of words to bind us so we speak directly, secretly. I want the idea of formulating a special message of speech, something just for us."

Ed agreed "I honestly do think that it's fascinating that with all the millions of descriptions and infinite English language available to us, to think somehow a tiny amount of letters or words can initiate the beginning of something incredible. Like a poet, sifting through an endless mass of further options, and deciding only the bare minimum, sourcing only the absolute essential to convey their meaning. It also does awaken the dormant Oxford spy in me that those Cambridge fellows always seemed to suggestively gloat over, though without ever confirmation, at our annual boat race."

"John Le Carre would be so impressed." Izzy murmured to Ed's story, as her gentle hands brushed through his strong sandy hair, tenderly. "So I'm giving us the challenge of three. Only three, and they must makes absolute sense and the intention be complete in its entirety. Do you see? Is this OK? Are you listening?" She leant in and began chuckling herself when reaching over to his ribs to tickle him into attention. Laughing as he nodded his acquiescent, pulling her small hands away from his torso, yet remaining them still in his.

Kissing her sensually, his tongue probing and intense, he continued just long enough to feel her nipples harden erotically like two smooth pebbles begging for their own attention as she pushed them further into his ever receptive chest. "I like the idea of us being connected in a private way, in every way, that you would want to say something only to me."

"Three words." She said, smirking before correcting herself. "Three words please," she insisted; despite her breathlessness, despite her reddening cheeks and wetness that he could touch with his insightful and meticulous fingers. His mouth that was on Izzy's neck, caressing her into sensual submission, moved upwards again to face her closely, their eyes once again connected, wanting and urgent.

Slowly Ed lifted his lips, getting as close to Izzy's left ear as possible, he spoke his three words.

"May. I. Feel?" He whispered conspiratorially and whilst he did so a strange emotion came upon him, desperation of hope that she'd decipher this code he was supplying. He had inadvertently set her up for a test which he was now anxious for her to pass. Those three titled words; three clues that could give them a whole future inventive, creative exchanges they could continue together all their days; proving that they shared something much more than others; an innate connection, a perfect soulful link.

A slight pause, a momentary click of remembered lines on a well-thumbed page turned into a slow moan of deep approval and with solving this personal puzzle, Izzy felt such a fierce rush of love for him, extending both from the acute shared intellect and her aroused willing body. The whole weight of her pulled down on to his very centre, enveloping perfectly his own hard shape within her soft openness as they let their physical actions continually answer his magnificent question. She replied,

"You. Are. Mine."

may I feel said he

(i'll squeal said she

just once said he)

it's fun said she

(may I touch said he

how much said she

a lot said he)

why not said she

(let's go said he

not too far said she

what's too far said he

where you are said she)

may **I stay** said he

(**wh**ich way said she

like this said he

if you kiss said she

may I move said he

is it love said she)

if you're willing said he

(but you're killing said she

but it's life said he

but your wife said she

now said he)

ow said she

(tiptop said he

don't stop said she

oh no said he)

go slow said she

(cccome? said he

ummm said she)

you're divine said he

(**you** are Mine said she)

may I feel, e e cummings

Chapter Eighteen

"Poetry heals the wounds inflicted by reason."

Novalis

After

The newly introduced poetry readings were to change Ed's life. Instead of accept fate, to agree to the trajectory of what life's road had taken, he began to assert an up-rise against it. To fight the powerlessness he had so recently worn like a fitted cape gathering him all around and holding him in, Ed had made a start to improve their circumstance in the best way he knew how. He knew could not change the past or stay living there. Remaining passive and unhappy was a choice he could live with either.

Of course Izzy still needed her hearing aids to listen, he knew this as fact. What Ed did not know, or ever could, was how much she was able to hear without them. Anything at all? A buzz? A whisper? An endless babbling noise? She never explained it to him. Hearing without her aids was something in their history that they hadn't got round to discussing. About certain medical issues from her past trauma she was very limited and concise, quite black and white in her delivery. Pain or none. In or out. Yes or no. The only grey area was the broken clay bowl between them, where the hearing implements sat.

On a call to Marcel one Friday at the office for their regular weekly updates on Izzy, they discussed how she had been all those years ago when she abandoned her words before.

"Oh goodness that was so very hard. We were just crazy ourselves at the time. Alex had lost his brother and sister-in-law, the only family he had left, so he was grief-stricken, desperately so. And of course we've never had any children of our own so to be in charge of a nine year old, a very traumatised one at that was incredibly daunting for us both. We loved Izzy though, that was never up for question. But when she arrived from the hospital to begin her life with us, she was a shell of a girl. Her eyes were so distant and far away. It was heart-breaking, really. I can still remember the pain of it all those years ago, even now."

"I think Alex said it was nearly two years it took her to come out of it again. Is that right? Did she ever talk about why she didn't speak? Was there any sort of medical or psychological explanation?" Ed asked. Two years seemed impossible, even though they were now already halfway through that timescale. But it was more than that. It wasn't simply how long it took but why that felt so important to him. Where did she go? What was she thinking about that stopped her from living there, in that moment, with him?

"We saw all sorts of doctors, physical, mental, emotional. Oxford is endlessly academic as you know, so Alex took it as his mission to consult and confer with them all. Tests were done, examinations taken. Mostly at home but I do recall going back and forth into the John Radcliffe for a while, but my honest recollection of what we concluded was she was simply 'gone' to a safe place in her head that she had created. There was some technical term, you must ask Alex he'd know it for sure, but essentially she lived elsewhere for a while. I suspect it was a place where her parents were still alive, in some form or another."

"She never talked about it to you both?" Ed questioned.

"Never. Not just to us but she didn't talk about it to anyone. It was miraculous really. One day she was lost in her head and her books, silence all around and then she came back to us. With just a few words, she spoke something about a great chapter and better stories and then Bam! She was with us again." Marcel spoke this part with a croak in his throat at the incredible moment they experienced so long ago.

"She did go from nothing, just in bed, motionless to moving her body around the upstairs of the building, sitting, walking, leaning against things. This then took her to books, reading the novels within reach of her, ones we had collected and placed in the hope she would choose to pick them up and explore. This opened up a real hunger for the literary world which by degrees opened her up again to the real world among us."

Remembering the brief conversation he had previously with her Uncle, about Izzy's childhood responses from the accident with her parents, 'I don't need them to read' Ed thought he could apply his new efforts to a two-way approach.

Ed had committed a lot of time to thinking about how to achieve the result he so desired, bringing his wife back to him, and once the first poetry week was almost up he felt sure he had chosen the right path. His confidence in all things had been affected for so long he already knew this was something he couldn't manage completely on his own. However what he also knew was, for most of his adult life he had been in a position of building up an assembly of people, clients, friends, fellows, who were the ideal choices to assist him with this brave new project. Ed had an inspired decision to go right back to the beginning. Like the diligent student he ever was, Ed researched, and referenced, accessed relevant information and eventually outsourced his new project to the very best experts he knew. This would be time. It would be now he would see if the world secret they decided nearly two decades before, was truly the solution he so very much wished for.

'Courage, dear heart.'

The Voyage of the Dawn Treader, C.S. Lewis

Chapter Nineteen

"I am sad and lonely. Lay your hands upon my mane

so that I can feel you are there and let us walk like that."

The Lion, the Witch and the Wardrobe, C.S. Lewis

After

Email; Geoffrey, Henry, Andrew, Ahmed, Richard, Ishmar, Juan

Re: Help

Dear Fellow Aslans,

I hope you don't mind me writing to you all on our group email. I'm aware it was only four months ago when we were all together for our annual event but since then I find myself in need of requesting your knowledgeable and expert assistance with a private matter.

As you know, Isobel and I have been going through rather a dark time of late and I have been at a loss as how to help us get through it.

Since that fateful talk by Henry so many years ago which began our monthly discussions, we must have sifted, selected, omitted and kept safe for later thousands if not more, poems. Only recently did it come to me that sharing some of the greater works, the more relevant, the familiar or the distracting and inspirational poetry we have uncovered over our decades, might be a way to do this.

I have begun with Auden (of course) but would very much appreciate a few of your own contributions as to which pieces or poets you each personally feel may be useful at such a time.

I know Geoffrey that you have been kind enough to pass on some of your comforting theological works but at this stark moment in my life, where so much seems pushed to the edge of the precipice, I find myself drawn time and again back to the world secret we awarded, and put my faith in the power of that for now.

Again, thank you so very much for your time and help with this. I look forward to reading your selections.

Ed

p.s. I may well come back to you Geoffrey if that's ok, if this new idea doesn't work out.

"Poetry at its best, is the language your soul would speak

if you could teach your soul to speak."

Jim Harrison

Chapter Twenty

"Love anything and your heart will be wrung and possibly broken. If you want to make sure of keeping it intact you must give it to no one, not even an animal. Wrap it carefully, round with hobbies and little luxuries; avoid all entanglements. Lock it up safe in the casket or coffin of your selfishness. But in that casket, safe, dark, motionless, airless, it will change. It will not be broken; it will become unbreakable, impenetrable, irredeemable. To love is to be vulnerable."

C. S. Lewis

After

Thursday 3/6

For the past year Ed had put a hold on his legendary Wilde lunches. Not only had he to get back in time for Izzy so trying to put a curfew on such a well organised and multi-peopled event seemed ungenerous and ill-mannered but he himself did not feel like attending let alone hosting such vibrant and upbeat occasions. He could in no way claim to suffer the enormity of grief the same way his wife had. His in comparison felt almost fraudulent and petty. He had no emotional vocabulary to untangle it.

Instead of Wilde lunches it was Thursday drinks with Carron, a new and unplanned replacement, but welcome none the less. Over their many years she had often been referred to as his 'Work Wife' amongst their closer clients or familiar members of the other Publishing houses they sometimes spent time with. It was a title they both laughed along at, quite the cliché, and an almost lazy summary of what the entirety of their now fifteen year friendship was.

In those initial first years of them both setting up Fallon House there was no time for either of them to pursue social and romantic lives as well as career ones. Fourteen hour days, each weekend taken over with mountains of manuscripts, sketches, notebooks and folders filled to capacity with new tales of old stories re-told, original takes on modern lives, imaginings on past historical events, Classics revisited and reviewed and everything besides. This was their haystack in the search for that literary treasured needle.

After those first thirty months of searching, scanning, re-checking and examining all types of Authors and their works, when the rent looked close to not being paid in the following weeks; after Ed and Carron's no payroll salary since month twenty one, they were flagging absolutely but refused to give up. Somewhere they knew within those sheets of A4, not just good writers, commercially viable novels or able essayists that they could cleverly market but that one solid nugget of gold that could blow them wide open, make their name matter and find their power in the wondrous Literary world. Discovering this star was every Editor, Agent and Publisher's dream.

It may well have never happened. The partnership was close to ending before those first three years were up, where they would have to admit defeat and go work for other reputable and more established companies. Their urgent searching and brilliant determination of this joint goal was something Ed did consider them to be like an unbreakable team, an extraordinary pair.

On finding that pivotal novel by Arthur Valentine, *In Time for Shelley*, those celebrations and relief, there was a small window in time where they could have followed on and taken their relationship further. Back then, in Carron's less decorated office, with two different armchairs and cheaper Whiskey, Ed watched in admiration this woman who knew him so well, who he trusted most in his life at that very moment, who shared thousands of pieces of beloved Literature and glorious quotations from favourite chapters and yet, yet, somehow the moment passed.

The rare times Ed thought about marriage, he always hoped somehow his true love would be a women who he could unite with his endless passion of books and the splendour of all language he so admired. That it would be the culmination of these beautiful things so close in his life, so very near his own heart, that would be his fate.

So why not Carron? Why not her? Surely their pairing was perfect? He thought, all those years ago. Maybe later, Ed had told himself. Don't do anything immediately; to upset the business that their hard work was beginning to reap and now grow into something they both dreamed of.

But somewhere deep inside of him he worried that if it was so right then nothing should have stopped him. If they were absolutely destined to be together then surely they would find a way to manage it, whenever and however.

He had also read enough romantic stories and poetry to see this wasn't always accurate or true to authentic life. You were always on the page, presented with an ideal and the theory was the point, not dragged down with the daily boredoms of details – though John Osbourne tried to show us. So often was romance tragic, cut short or at too great a cost. Yet from all his reading and learning from such plays and tales a small part of him remained that eternal romantic despite the realities, a love so substantial and fantastical it was only worthy and possible inside the paperback covers: That unachievable aspiration.

Perhaps it was timing, Ed left it at that answer. Maybe they were two partners that needed to wait. Maybe theirs would be ready for another time. Yeats spoke about the world being so full of magical things patiently waiting for our senses to grow sharper. This could be one of those, Ed had wondered. That same room, so long ago now.

It was only two hours after work, at those armchairs, with that amber spirit shared between them. Five thirty till seven thirty in the evening. If Ed left by then he would still be back within the hour to feed himself and Izzy at a reasonable time. It unsettled him how relaxed he was becoming in this safe space. It unnerved him at how much he had been looking forward to this weekly respite, this relief from duties. It almost felt as if his old life existed within these four familiar walls, before the baby, before Izzy, before Arthur

Valentine even, those days of freedom and possibility at the time he had been so work distracted he had not fully appreciated.

"The Man Booker winner was such a great choice this year. I met him a few weeks ago at the Agent's birthday drinks at the Savoy: Fascinating chap, such an interesting family history." Carron began. It was a book she knew they both enjoyed. With her forensic eye for writing and tone it was sometimes hard for Carron to relax and read for pleasure so used she was to being observant for flaws to correct or a style to further polish from her own Authors.

"Did I hear somewhere his father had discovered an Island years ago? Off the Scandinavian coast?" Ed enquired. The theme of the celebrated story was based on an intrepid explorer and his encounters with places and cultures across the planet.

"Yes, now there would be a diary I would wish to purchase. He commanded a boat with a crew team of three, and managed to travel all over the globe skirting the beaches and shores as their base line. I think they began by taking samples for scientific research which funded the travels but they ended up with far greater findings as they went on." Carron loved reading about travel and foreign places. She herself had asked to be in charge of that specific genre for Fallon to incorporate her own interest with the business one. Meeting the people who wrote these journals and memoirs was one of her favourite parts of working. Without the lifestyle to spend travelling the planet herself, by default she felt she learnt through their evocative descriptions and clearly-explained events through the eyes of such writers. That personal filter they saw the world through felt a privilege for her to share. Reading these was what Poetry was to Ed. This was what she believed touched so deeply inside her, that universal connectivity, belonging to a greater state than alone.

Their easy conversation carried on, it was light and comfortable. For Ed it was simple in its joy, the returned voice of another. That dialogue, two people responding and reacting to the everyday. He hadn't realised how loud that silence in his home truly was: How one could feel so lost in a house even when everything was familiar and yours.

They continued talking and sipping the very fine Whiskey. When the clock on the wall reached half past seven Ed almost stayed on. The weightlessness of self, the natural use of smiling and even laughing throughout Carron's gentle and entertaining anecdotes was what felt like the cool, fresh breath of air he had needed through such hot and humid journey.

He got himself up and they said their goodbyes, back to work again tomorrow. Ed found he truly did not want to leave but he did.

Carron did not want him to go either.

If she was honest, she never did.

"Still there's no denying that in some sense I 'feel better', and with that comes at once a sort of shame, and a feeling that one is under a sort of obligation to cherish and torment and prolong one's unhappiness."
A Grief Observed, C. S. Lewis

Chapter Twenty-One

"For all the sad words of tongue and pen,
the saddest are these 'it might have been'."
John Greenleaf Whittier

After

Thursday 3/6

Ed was late home. Izzy looked at her watch again, six fifty-five. Izzy lay there, her stomach unsettled. She wanted to get up and check through the window if there was an obvious reason for this. Had he got caught speaking to a neighbour walking from the Tube? Was there a delay in public transport maybe? Had he fallen on a curb? Or worse, mugged? Involved in an accident? Was he our there injured? How would she know? Despite her racing mind her body remained inactive, unwilling to commit to standing up, so heavy it felt from the burden of its daily maternal imagination.

Nausea began creeping up her neck and into the wideness of her closed mouth. It tasted sour and fetid; it tasted of rumoured panic and the nervousness of oncoming menace. Why wasn't he back yet? Her husband wasn't a man who was ever late.

The child of her mind was playing quietly with a half blown up, red balloon on the rug beside her, humming a sweet tune. It was from a childhood rhyme Izzy had been teaching her earlier that day, Oranges and Lemons, one of her favourites.

Izzy was distracted. Instead of being absorbed in watching the beautiful actions of their little girl she couldn't concentrate for the restlessness that was unsettling her brain; the questions, the worry. Where could he have got to? Their daughter would be getting tired and she didn't want to say goodnight to her until Ed was home. It was only by their together-kiss that she was happy enough to send her off till the next day. Only on his return could she sign off her parental duties and slip back into the vague reality of 'real' life.

But now the usually comforting nursery music slowly started to feel slightly unnerving as it began getting bit louder and louder, opening out into the empty lounge, all from the tiny vocal chords of the charming toddler playing contentedly with her scarlet saggy toy. The large, empty room was, little by little, being swollen up acoustically by this infant's noise. It drowned out the clock ticking over the mantle, over took the rain drumming onto the window panes, raised itself higher than the much wanted but not occurring click and thud of the front door.

Izzy couldn't stop swallowing. It was a tightening of her throat, restricting her breathing into shallow gasps, as if the song out loud was removing air from all around it. She looked down at the little girl innocently singing away, happily. The red balloon in the chubby little hands seemed plumper now, larger than it had before. Her big green eyes glanced back up to her mother's and she giggled joyously, continuing her melody.

Where was Ed? Izzy checked her watch again. The balloon was getting bigger now. Izzy could see the rubber edges, once slack with loose pockets now smoothed firm and taut as the oxygen within it pushed the inside space further and further away from its centre. It felt as though it was somehow siphoning off the air all around them and feeding it into itself. The air was being stolen. Not that their little girl noticed, she simply carried on as before but her face picked up an wondrous gaze, as her tune picked up momentum with the expansion of the growing red balloon she kept hold of in her sticky, kiddy grasp.

As if in tandem, Izzy's light breaths became sharper and shallower as the scarlet rubber orb pulsed deeper and fuller. Her head became dizzier and she felt faint, she had the sensation as if she would collapse and fold into herself twisted and empty like those withered tubes of oil paint she'd find littering the floors in the Rectory art room near her mother's old studio.

Izzy's daughter looked over at her now, the small, toddler eyes widening in concern at how anxious her mother looked. She was not used to her seeming worried and fretful. She saw how her hands wrung over and across themselves in an effort to soothe, how her body began rocking forwards and backwards rhythmically, getting faster and faster as if she was in pain.

Izzy's lungs felt hot and swollen, the air around seemed weak and far away. Watching the balloon get bigger and bigger she could almost see the trail of wind from her shallow breaths being suctioned out and into the expanding balloon.

The child stopped her singing but the song continued on, she did not know where. It was becoming louder and upsetting. She was becoming tearful. She did not like what was happening at all. The growing red toy was pulling at her hand trying to move into the space between the two of them. She couldn't see her Mummy anymore because of the large balloon. It was blowing up so big that she couldn't get passed it to go to her. They were both trapped either side of this enormous stretching scarlet rubber that was already touching the ceiling as well as filling out across-ways, extending out to each side of the walls: Ever growing, ever creeping towards them more.

Izzy wanted to shout to her daughter but as in life, no words came out. She could silently, desperately, mouth to her, unseen, but she remained mute. Just the tune of the nursery rhyme played louder and louder in her ears, drowning out all other senses; making the balloon speed up to the pace of the verses yet it seemed to be stuck now on one part, over and over it repeated, over and over, like the hand-pumps used to inflate toys, pushing and pulling, harder and tighter. *Here comes a candle to light you to bed. And here comes a chopper to chop off your head. Chop off your head. Chop off your head. Chop off your head.* Faster and faster, louder and louder. *Chop off your head. Chop off your head. Chop off your…* Whirl. Click. Close.

BANG!!!!!!!!!!!!!!!!!!!!!!!!!!!!!!!!!!!

Ed shut the door behind him as he strode up the few stairs in front, his satchel heavy with the books and novels within it. A slick of rain upon his hair and coat from the beginning of a thunder storm he almost avoided. In the semi-dark hallway he began his usual walk towards the lounge.

Before Izzy knew what had happened she gasped at seeing the many specks of random red latex confetti rain down upon the room covering herself and all surfaces in the exploded toy. The trembling child, viewing her mother clearly again from where she had crouched in fear by the edge of the coffee table, ran over through the many shapes of falling colour and pushed herself strong and shaking into the warm and welcoming arms of Izzy.

The rhyme ended also at the popping of the balloon, with the unlatching of the door which now left a haunting lack of any noise save the sobbing of the tiny girl, her little chest rising up and down in broken muffled cries, her face pressed against her mother's seeking comfort and love. Izzy's neck tucked down, her arms clasping tight this precious person. Izzy's hands held gently upon soft curly hair and she felt her own cheeks wet with her daughter's tears which quickly turned into her own.

Ed walked over, as he ever did, towards his wife, her back still to him, her body folded up holding herself in a close embrace as if, he thought, she was trying to keep warm. Getting closer Ed picked up the blanket from the bottom of the long chair and opened it out. He placed it very carefully over her shoulders and along her knees, hoping to help.

He leant in as always, to kiss her head, to say hello and to tell her he was home. His heart sank a little as he once again did not know if she really noticed him, or if she did, would rather he had not returned. He sighed a little as he watched her a moment, lost to him. He felt for a fragile second as if he should stay beside her a little longer today. There seemed something in the gap between them that precise instant that he sensed was needed but unsure what, like a forgotten flavour or the act of remembering an old dream.

It could of course be nothing, he told himself, just that desperate, wishful thinking. Just his own imagination, he thought, pushing the possibility away as he began to leave the room towards the kitchen. He was already late to make their supper.

Izzy lay frozen. Her arms closed but empty. Her face streaked with quiet crying. Her breath steady now so as not to incite questions or explanation, answers that she didn't want to tell.

That bird above had watched it all. He had heard the music and its sadness fly up and into his glass shell as if it were longing. He hurt for the motionless-lady who never stirred but could see through her mind all of her daytime ghosts as bright and clear as if watching a play. He hurt for that ever-changing girl who was never allowed to leave; that young soul who never had any peace even though she had already died. And his own tender heart broke for that strong husband below who loved the woman still alive beside him that felt like his real-life ghost.

"At other times it feels like being mildly drunk or concussed. There is a sort of invisible blanket between the world and me. I find it hard to take in what anyone says. Or perhaps, hard to want to take it in. It is so uninteresting. Yet I want the others about me. I dread the moments when the house is empty. If only they would talk to one another and not to me."

A Grief Observed, C. S. Lewis

Silence – Billy Collins

There is the sudden silence of the crowd

above the player not moving on the field,

and the silence of the orchid.

The silence of the falling vase

before it strikes the floor,

the silence of the belt when it is not striking the child.

The stillness of the cup and the water in it,

the silence of the moon

and the quiet of the day far from the roar of the sun.

The silence when I hold you to my chest,

the silence of the window above us,

and the silence when you rise and turn away.

And there is the silence of this morning

which I have broken with my pen,

a silence that had piled up all night

like snow falling in the darkness of the house –

the silence before I wrote a word

and the poorer silence now.

Chapter Twenty–Two

"Poetry gives us courage and sets us straight with the world.

Poems are great companions and friends."

David Whyte

After

Dr Ahmed Pohv

11, Richmond Park

London

E4 6YP

Dear Edward,

Forgive me for replying your email with this paper version but I do so feel when sending a poem it is the handheld version that holds the most striking impact. I think I know you well enough that you also agree.

I was sorry to hear about Isobel and your troubles, having never married or had a family myself as you know, I feel I am a little under qualified to comment or advise save for just my absolute best wishes and hopes for a kinder future for you both.

As we have been privileged enough to have read so many wonderful poems over the years it is of course very difficult task to distil all this into a singular piece but this is what they are written for. The solace, the comfort, the universal longings are why they remain as imperative as they do. Canon Reuben taught us that above all other teachings and I for one couldn't be more indebted.

I include my choice here. In literary terms I believe it would come under the entitlement of 'Moving On' that ominous and really quite dreadful clichéd phrase but the intention of it, I trust you find, is pure enough.

I also include my own copy of the Lewis' "The Problem of Pain", which I would be grateful if you kept and perhaps called on in later days. I know it was an enormous support to me in those hard months following the death of my parents all those years ago now.

I look forward to seeing you in a next year for the Aslan meet but please don't hesitate to call on me further if you need anything else from me before then, anything at all.

Yours faithfully,

Ahmed

"The inmost spirit of poetry, in other words, is at bottom, in every recorded case, the voice of pain – and the physical body, so to speak, of poetry, is the treatment by which the poet tries to reconcile that pain with the world."

Ted Hughes

Since I Have Felt the Sense of Death by Helen Hoyt

Since I have felt the sense of death,

      Since I have borne it's dread, its fear –

      Oh, how my life has grown more dear

Since I have felt the sense of death!

Sorrows are good, and cares are small,

Since I have known the loss of all.

Since I have felt the sense of death,

      And death forever at my side –

      Oh, how the world has opened wide

Since I have felt the sense of death!

My hours are jewels that I spend,

For I have seen the hours end.

Since I have felt the sense of death,

      Since I have looked on that black night –

      My inmost brain is fierce with light

Since I have felt the sense of death.

O dark, that made my eyes to see!

Oh death, that gave my life to me!

Chapter Twenty-Three

> "Where you used to be, there is a hole in the world, which I find myself constantly walking around in the daytime, and falling in at night."
>
> Edna St. Vincent Millay

After

Friday 3/6

Izzy woke with a start and ran out of bed. The bathroom door was ajar and she carefully pushed it, afraid as to what she would see when it swung open fully. But swiftly, before cowardice took over, she turned on the light above. She stared at the empty bath tub, white and clean with overwhelming relief. Her nightmare image of a tiny baby's body lying under a bath full of water, its bloody, torn umbilical cord gently moving back and forth with the lapping flow was still fresh in her mind as the dream's hateful chill could be felt from the bedroom behind, still trying to catch her up.

She walked over to the tub and placed her hands firmly down touching all around the base, sides and ledges to confirm without question, that what she had previously envisioned was no longer true; empty, ceramic, cold; even though the bitter taste of fear was still ever present upon her tongue.

The low repeated thud of the window's vibrations, not closed hours before, could be felt in the quiet darkness. It was coming from the front room as Izzy turned off the bathroom light and went to attend it.

The pale curtain was flapping furiously in the breeze as the metal hook in the frame pulled and pushed against itself in rhythm with the outside elements. Unclasping the casement she stood for a moment staring up at the dark night sky, feeling a smattering of rain spray over her like sea foam. Her body wired from the frenzied visions that had awoken her so rapidly, and although her breathing was now calmer, her muscles had seized tight into anxious knots from her shoulders to her ankles, a paralysing sensation, only slightly soothed by the gentle damp splashing upon her from the midnight storm.

"Izzy. Izzy." He called to her from the doorframe. His hair bed-tousled and his eyes bleary with the hour. "Everything ok?" he spoke and signed with his hands at the same time. He briefly glanced into the bowl and saw, as always, her hearing aids so he did not continue talking to her in words out loud.

She looked over to him, her face glistening like glitter as the moonlight shone in and he heard himself gasp at how beautiful she was, right there, in that moment. It had been so long since she had looked directly at him, he hadn't realised just how powerful such eye contact truly was. It felt electric in its charge, intense in that now they were locked in each other's sight, something had to be actioned. It would feel just too sad if either had simply looked away.

Her grassy green eyes held his gaze and Ed, surprised in its occurrence, welcomed it gladly. His body craved hers so entirely that he could do nothing else but think of her in his arms again. It was too much to wish for, his expectations had lowered so much along this torturous journey of theirs, but with a bravery he didn't quite know he could marshal, breath-takingly slowly he took a small, steady step towards her, gradual and soft, so as not to startle her to break this moment. And he then waited. Staying still and wary, like watching a solitary small child on the opposite side of the road, as a fast car approaches oblivious, unable to know if the child will stay safe or run out into that dangerous path. In the charged space between them Izzy remained still and continued watching him. Her eyes seeming to will him something he had yet to interpret.

Stepping towards her further, slowly, ever slowly, his right hand now very gently moved up to his own lips. His flattened palm towards him touched there briefly before arching forward a few inches ahead. *Please,* he signed. Once again he repeated with his hand gesture, *Please.*

Izzy's eyes widened with the translation and without conscious intent, her shoulders softened and her arms loosened out from their tense clasp.

Ed perceived a change in the atmosphere before him, uncertain at first if he was correct or just wishing it so, regardless he softly stepped one pace further, almost near enough to touch her now and his kind, gentle eyes, those same ones she had fallen in love with so long ago, burrowed pleadingly into her own and his generous, soft lips mouthed the same earlier sentiment. *Please.*

And it was Izzy who now replied, quiet and perfect, with her own slight hands pressing against her wet skin. Her left palm was opened out flat and her right hand made a small fist with her thumb raised up. She continued to look towards him as her hand glided smoothly from close towards her and out to the further part of her palm. *Help,* she wrote then looking back at him to check he had seen it. *Help,* she made again.

Ed watched her hands and knew from the delicate swan-like form she was moving to make, exactly what she signed. Izzy's huge eyes glistened and pleaded to him, aware that she honestly did not know what would happen to her if he did not understand.

That glass bird's wire was as taut as it had ever been. The weight of all Izzy's grief was swiftly rising to the surface, perhaps ready in the hope to break out and share towards him or if unrequited, like a backdraft, inhaling out all the oxygen around it and rushing back into the vessel it was once contained, consuming it entirely. There was no way that fragile glass could keep it safely in. It wasn't possible that wire could support all that pain anymore.

And without further thought or challenge Ed reached out and collected her delicate hands in his and pressed them up to his face. The very touch of her skin on his, after so long felt euphoric, like a wondrous heavenly offering. The smell of her fingertips, the pressing of her cold, metallic wedding ring against his cheek was the most precious metal he had ever sensed. Eventually he moved her hands down, still held firm within his own and he placed his head upon hers; their foreheads touching, as they ever used to. Her cold damp skin pressed into his warm, pale face as he gently let go of her fingers so he could raise his arms wide open and enclose her safely within them. Her ear tucked on his chest so his heartbeat continually drumming, all the way through her molten body, the most beautiful sound she knew.

The glass bird that had previously twisted and spun as fierce as that sodden, wind-thrown curtain behind them, gently settled itself into a tiny rocking pulse. It's delicate shell. The bearing wire thinned out from all the previous panicked movements to an almost invisible line. It couldn't be long until it snapped. Not much longer now.

"I don't feel any pain
A little fall of rain
Can hardly hurt me now
You're here that's all I need to know
And you will keep me safe
And you will keep me close
And the rain will make the flowers grow."

Les Miserables

"...I like for you to be still

And you seem far away

It sounds as though you are lamenting

A butterfly cooing like a dove

And you hear me from far away

And my voice does not reach you

Let me come and be still in your silence

And let me talk to you with your silence

That is bright as a lamp

Simple, as a ring

You are like the night

With its stillness and constellations

Your silence is that of a star

As remote and candid..."

Pablo Neruda

Chapter Twenty–Four

"The more often (a person) feels without acting, the less he will be able ever to act,
and, in the long run, the less he will be able to feel."

C. S. Lewis

After

Waiting in case Izzy would panic and retreat back into the silent limbo place she leaves him for, Ed stood statue still. Her in his enclosed arms felt such a miraculous moment he needed to be sure he was not still asleep and dreamt it.

'Help' she had signed him, 'Help'. Thinking about this there and then, he felt it was his responsibility to do just what she asked of him. Trying to master a semblance of confidence he once had with her, Ed tried to remain calm and decide what to do next.

Izzy was stood into him, her clothes and skin slightly damp. He could feel the cold wind travel through the room with the open window and he worried she would catch a chill. Moving ever so slowly he reached his right arm across and behind her and shut the window closed. The wet curtain fell back into line just leaving a thin sliver free to expose the outside moonlight, bathing them both in its cool, silver shade.

Izzy had stayed close to him for a few minutes now and Ed felt able to gently walk them back into the bedroom so as to get her warm again and in dry clothes, without fear she would pull away. Switching the side lamp on he placed her carefully onto the edge of the bed where she sat, shoulders low and eyes looking down towards his ever-sturdy hands. Despite her stooped body language, a subtle shift could be felt from the air around her, a sort of wakefulness, a small sense of endeavour.

Ed opened his top drawer and removed a folded t-shirt. It was an old item, a navy college top from his University days. It was fraying at the sleeve ends and had some tiny holes appearing towards the neck seam but for the last few years Izzy had refused to let him throw it away. She was not a hoarder or collector of many past things but she had always been sentimental with certain items; mostly those that had a connection to their history together. The 'real beginning of her life', she would tell to him, on important dates, on birthdays and anniversaries, on rainy Sunday mornings and in small post-it notes she would leave on the fridge after too much dinner party red wine. *Before.*

Lifting the white cotton nightdress over her perfect glossy shoulders, Ed's heart skipped as he could see the almost full naked form of his adored wife. It had been so long. She was thinner than he remembered. Her breasts were smooth yet full, their rounded sides cupping beautifully by the slight weight of them, as they held up the dark nipples in front. Her upper ribs were visible underneath, in spite of Ed and the Boys' efforts in feeding her regularly, her frame was skinny and hollow. Just above the top of her white lace knickers the long scribble of that harsh, red scar was there, like a raw weld, a burn, the poppy-coloured mark to serve as a perpetual reminder, as if forgetting was even possible.

She knew he had seen it. Izzy felt his eyes on that shameful stripe as if he had touched it. She hated what it represented, why it was caused, but equally loved that it meant she had held their baby once behind it, that she had been a mother, if only for a short while.

Ed paused with the blue t-shirt ready to put her in it. He could sense he was losing Izzy again to that unknown place, how in a beat her self seemed to think about something away from right here and Ed was desperate for her not to disappear. Kneeling down in front of her so his face was closer again he pulled the familiar top over Izzy's head and she slowly put her arms through like an obedient child. She took a second to recognise his choice of clothing and then her mind returned back again into the space they were now sharing. The worn fabric supple from years of repeated washing felt safe to wear, as she had so often done those years before. And her eyes looked up to meet his again in wordless gratitude.

He moved towards her so their foreheads touched and his hands raised up to pull her long chestnut hair out of the t-shirt, and over down her back again. The large curls fell in between his strong fingers and he brushed them through the strands tenderly. He could feel her brow furrow on his own as her body instinctively responded to his closeness. Her lips opened and a sweet, breathy sigh pushed out touching his. Ed's eyes closed briefly in blissful reply.

Unsure of what he needed to do next he waited a moment to consider what was best. He didn't want to rush Izzy into anything. It had been so long since they were intimate in any way he was sure that initiating that, even though his whole body desperately wanted to, was too much right now. He didn't want to frighten her. He didn't want to make a mistake; just being this close again after so long was far more than he'd ever dared imagine.

Leaning back, Ed gently lifted Izzy's legs up so she was fully onto the bed and then tenderly pulled up the sheets over her. Turning the lamp off, he walked over to the other side of the bed. He was aware her eyes were watching all he did, waiting to know what he would do next, what he needed her to do. She had no notion of opinion or imposition. She felt empty of thought and action. All she wanted was to be shown what it was she had to know, be, consider. She was exhausted, tired down to the very core of her bones and everything felt like re-learning.

Ed climbed into bed beside Izzy. It was very early morning and his alarm would be going off in less than five hours. Whatever bad dreams and night time panics that woke Izzy earlier had now settled and she lay quietly still, her eyes heavy lidded, trying to blink away the drowsiness. Her head resting on the pillow next to him appeared calm and peaceful. Her hands placed between them both. He gathered them into his own lovingly and lightly kissed them. Her warm palms cradled his face softly like a caught falling snowflake, and before he could wish her goodnight she had fallen asleep, her breath lightly purring, her limbs at last loose and free.

Ed spent a minute reflecting on what had just happened and braved himself, for one fragment of a moment, feel a feather of hope float deep down inside him somewhere and settle briefly before it vanished. The last thing he remembered going round his brain before he drifted off was the curious thought that birds made of glass don't have feathers.

"Each lover has some theory of his own
About the difference between the ache
Of being with his love, and being alone:

Why what, when dreaming, is dear flesh and bone
That really stirs the senses, when awake,
Appears a simulacrum of his own.

Narcissus disbelieves in the unknown;
He cannot join his image in the lake
So long as he assumes he is alone.

The child, the waterfall, the fire, the stone,
Are always up to mischief, though, and take
The universe for granted as their own.

The elderly, like Proust, are always prone
To think of love as a subjective fake;
The more they love, the more they feel alone.

Whatever view we hold, it must be shown

Why every lover has a wish to make

Some kind of otherness his own:

Perhaps, in fact, we are never alone."

Are You There? W. H. Auden

Chapter Twenty–Five

"So Matilda's strong young mind continued to grow; nurtured by the voices of all those authors who had sent their books out into the world like ships on the sea. These books gave Matilda a hopeful and comforting message: You are not alone."

Roald Dahl

Before

Each work leaves an invisible stroke of a new shade within them both, leaving behind from the learnings of those other's words. These shared written pieces uniting them, creating a secret colour inside, completely unique and original, like the overlapping of the handmade tissue papers from the Gallery piece they had loved and bought.

Those early dating days created endless ways of finding exciting connections from the very ordinary, making small pathways of their very own into everyday customaries. It knotted them invisibly closer and gave a privacy from the outside world. Perhaps that was the very point.

It was her Uncle Alex that had given Izzy the novel *The God of Small Things* by Arundhati Roy for her twenty-sixth birthday. The front cover depicting a muted green photo of lily pads in water resting beautifully by the bright pinks of the flower poised underneath the title lay like the bud of an opening mouth ready to kiss. The pale letters on the darker background shades appeared elegant and tender, a whisper of colour in the middle of the page as if placed directly on the water, so slight as if it would disappear softly back into the pond behind it, evaporated like a breath.

Ed being usually blessed with a stern constitution was hardly ever ill yet the winter in their first year together he had been taken with severe bronchitis and had spent a blurry week at his flat with Izzy taking care of him whilst he dozed, drifted and recovered in a daze of anti-biotics and stabilising temperatures.

She would fix him broth soups and make him strong mint tea with honey. She helped wash him and dress him in clean sweatshirts and pyjama bottoms when he had sweated with fever. She would warm him kindly with a hot, wet towelling cloth on his icy brow when the cold flashes hit, tucking more blankets over him despite the creaking old radiator blasting out tropical, fiery heat.

Ed remembered little of those truly poorly seven days save for one particular part. Her small slender body perched alongside him on the temporary bed-couch trying not to cause him discomfort or be too close as to feel she was taking away some of the air around him that his tense, wheezing chest so desperately at times needed to gather all in.

She lay as close as she dared so even in his brittle and clouded sleep he would register he was not alone, and she would read to him, not knowing if he could understand or recall at later days. She would read out loud in her soft and clear voice, lilting her vowels and looping her sentence pace so as to infer action or sorrow. She read out loud to imprint the words she saw on the paper through his perfect ears and creep into his leaden brain, projecting the author's story so directly and imposingly it was as if he was watching it on a bright screen from his own imagining; so beautifully it was written, so lucidly the characters and tale was told.

"'…As she leaned against the door in the darkness, she felt her dream, her afternoon-mare move inside her like a rib of water rising from the ocean, gathering into a wave, The cheerful one-armed man with salty skin and a shoulder that ended abruptly like a cliff emerged from the shadows of the jagged beach and walked towards her.

Who was he?

Who could he have been?

The God of Loss.

The God of Small Things.

The God of Goose Bumps and Sudden Smiles.

He could only do one thing at a time.

If he touched her, he couldn't talk to her, if he loved her

he couldn't leave, if he spoke he couldn't listen, if he fought

he couldn't win.

Ammu longed for him. Ached for him with the whole of her

biology…."'

Izzy read one of her favourite works to him not knowing how precious it would be, almost-asleep, almost-awake. It was their shared love of literature that brought them close on that first day and now, months later, it proved to be working again to tighten them further in like a broken bone seeking its matching fractured part, time taken too quietly and invisibly to the human eye, heal strongly together. The power of books and words to them was medicine. It was their joint faith.

Little did they know in those joyful, timeless, early days how this would be tested. They were yet to see how cruel life could be even to those that do not seem to deserve it.

Before they had the chance for more loving years. Before the bird watched above them. *Before, before.*

So he lay there contented, like a small child, as she read and she read and she read. Novels, novellas, her favourites and ones she thought he might not have known yet, so much was her own knowledge from the family shop and others she thought he might want to hear again: timeless ones, stories that mean newer things in later years as you have lived a little longer. She started with *The God of Small Things,* and continued with *Down All the Days, The Unpleasantness at the Bellona Club, The Problem of Pain, A Moveable Feast, The Summer Book* and finally *The Iron Man,* Ed's own copy; the one he was reading when they first met. It was such a soulful tale. How Izzy felt for that solitary metal hero: how she remembered so long ago of her childhood being alone in that dark.

It was a bright Saturday December morning when the fever finally broke and Ed's lungs felt freer and clean again. He woke slowly about nine o'clock, his eyes adjusted foggy to sharp as he focused on Izzy's coffee cup resting on the small table in front of him. For the first time since he had taken ill the smell was appealing and delicious, not bitter and nauseating. He guessed it was her second cup of the day by a few settled drip marks on the higher rim as this newer brew was still steaming with its fresh warmth lifting out of the top.

Iz lay beside him, as always, her cold small feet slightly hooking round onto his muscular back shins, tucking in to gather his body heat upon them. She was still reading to him but softly now so as to be of comfort and not to wake. She had reached the ending of it, that final paragraph so familiar to Ed he had read it himself so many times to have been permanently inscribed in his memory like a tattoo. As she continued the tale Ed joined in, his exacting match to each line written. They spoke it together like a beloved song or a well-worn prayer.

"…And the space-bat-angel's singing had the most unexpected effect. Suddenly the world became wonderfully peaceful. The singing got inside everybody and made them as peaceful as starry space, and blissfully above all their earlier little squabbles. The strange soft eerie space-music began to alter all the people of the world. They stopped making weapons. The countries began to think how they could live pleasantly alongside each other, rather than how to get rid of each other. All they wanted to do was have peace to enjoy this strange, wild, blissful music from the giant singer in space…"

There was a pause between them as Izzy smiled widely and warmly towards him acknowledging with relief his improved health, happy in his awareness of the now. She carefully placed the book down onto the table and leaned in to him, faces close, noses almost touching, their eyes locked in a quiet gratitude of one another.

"I. Missed. You." She whispered. Her fingers squeezed his palm lightly with each of the three words; their favourite number. His firm arms shifted open to hold her tighter in.

"Sun. Moon. Stars." He replied into her hair, his hand stroking her back as he said each one.

Sighing happily into his cosy chest Izzy waited a tiny moment to simply listen to the strong, whooshing beat of his beautiful heart. Perhaps it was her wishing it but at that precise moment she could swear it was tapping to the pulse of three; Boom-boom-boom. Boom-boom-boom. Boom-boom-boom.

Ed lifted her head gently towards his and they started kissing. Tender and delicate at first to test his strength after so long infirmed, but leading then into longer and passionate moments, lips pressed and fervent, tongues licking and lapping, twisting themselves together like recollected streams falling into itself, curled and repeated. It ended into being a very good day.

That winter of Ed's illness was so many years ago now, but back then it was a lovely memory made. Something Ed had, despite his ailed condition, regardless of how vague real world and time felt in that miasma of pill prescription and lost days, he had never forgotten her compassion to him and without him having to ask, the way she tended him back to health in the best way he could wish for. That wasn't just love that was their love, not only perfect but a perfection unique to them. This was surely the beginning of their very own story.

silently if, out of not knowable
night's utmost nothing, wanders a little guess
(only which is this world) more of my life does
not leap than with the mystery your smile

sings of if (spiralling as luminous
they climb oblivion)voices who are dreams
less into heaven certainly earth swims
than each my deeper death becomes your kiss

losing through you what seemed myself;I find
selves unimaginably mine;beyond
sorrows own joys and hoping's very fears

yours in the light by which my spirit's born.
yours is the darkness of my soul's return
-    you are my sun, my moon and all of my stars

#38, ee cummings

Chapter Twenty-Six

"Poetry is what in a poem makes you laugh, cry, prickle, be silent, make your toe nails twinkle, makes you do this or that or nothing, makes you know that you are alone in the unknown world, that your bliss and suffering is forever shared and forever all your own."

Dylan Thomas

After

To: Ed, Fallon House

CC:

Re: Help

Hi there Ed,

Sorry things don't seem to be better since we last spoke. Cathy has tried to be in touch with Izzy, phone messages, texts, notes in the post etc., but obviously she's not up to replying to people at the moment. Am sure Cathy will keep on trying. It's difficult as being pregnant herself and what you guys went through she's very aware it's perhaps not the best timing for her to visit for Izzy's sake. If you can pass on to how much she is often in our thoughts and prayers - you both are - we would be very thankful.

I went back through the selections of poems I have. I looked specifically for the purpose you requested and thought maybe it would be better to start afresh and find a new piece that we haven't discussed between us and could be unknown to a few. Thankfully there are still living poets out there writing away, though goodness knows how they make a living. Not sure any of them ever do, even Auden confessed to so much, as it wasn't the writing of poems but more the employment of talking about doing so that paid his way.

Anyway, well done with beginning with Wystan, he is truly King of them all in my opinion. My mother-in-law still talks about your reading of his at our wedding. About the only part she did actually enjoy according her to face in the photos but will leave it there.

I'll call you next week and we could try and get that lunch in we keep talking about.

Wishing you so much luck my friend. All the best,

Juan

p.s. I have a feeling Cathy might be in touch with her own version of a helpful poem. This is what comes with marrying an American I suppose. No reserved emotions safely squirrelled away like us British are trained to do, perhaps her way is best. I hope you don't mind. There's no stopping her once she's set her mind to something and she does so think the world of you both.

"Poetry is eternal graffiti written in the heart of everyone."
Lawrence Ferlinghetti

Words fall short

To express a sense of loss

It can only be felt

in the emptiness it left.

In the longing of your heart,

in some chamber of your soul,

for a dear one gone

in a flash, we are forever apart.

In the silent tears

that flow down your cheeks,

soaking the pillow case

as you lie curled up in bed.

In the half smile

that never reaches your eyes.

The voids that fills you

and makes you wonder why you are alive.

With time the ache becomes dull,

and from time to time

you find yourself awake

tossing, turning going down

the memory lane,

some sweet sense of pain.

You are never whole.

As long as there is a longing

in your soul.

In time you realise

you have to let it go,

and make peace

and deal with grief.

Finally when it does,

you grow wise

compassionate and loving

and gain a new insight

into life that is a mystery.

Chapter Twenty–Seven

"You don't have a soul.

You are a soul.

You have a body."

C. S. Lewis

After

"So Ed, you have been working alongside the Poet Laureate this last year, could you perhaps tell us where your love of this particular subject came from?"

"Of course, it's one I know almost precisely down to not simply the year and date but time and context as well. When I spent my years studying here in Oxford amidst our expected arrogance of youth, we created a club, as boys like to do; specifically a debating group that was formed purposefully to try and convince the rest of us why their chosen studies in relation to the world, was the most definitive and fundamental one; 'What is the Secret to the Greatest Life.' Those younger years contain an almost nuclear level of nervous wonder, a knight's quest for knowledge and desperation to belong; effectively, quite a useful combination for trying to get stuff done.

We called ourselves 'The Aslans', terrible name of course, but what else do us Lewis fandoms do. Being the initial creator I was exempt from speaking but rather placed in the position of a conduit of order, an administrative referee I suppose, which isn't a million miles away from my future career, hanging on those coat tails from the work-clever others. I always did find it fascinating hitching one's wagon onto another genius' star.

Anyway, I digress, the point is we chose scholars to represent each subject, Mathematics, Physics, Medical, Literature, Religion, History etc, there was twenty- six of us in all and we were to meet twice a month in a clandestine venue. We began by choosing one member to give a brief half an hour's talk, not a lecture, though that's clearly what it was. We had thought ourselves far too urbane and revolutionary; pushing ourselves so far away from the traditional old Dons to call it such.

Well, it was a riot of discussion, shouting, pleading, heckling I seem to remember, laughing a lot, but incredibly insightful and there were many occasions when some of us, upon hearing certain talks given with such passion and erudite convictions, were almost tempted to convert from our own subject's belief.

Most took it very seriously. Andrew had four-way colour pie charts, Richard had made a table top size helix sculpture, Juan printed off signed copies of his personal presentation, Ishmar had quite a lot of things laminated and Geoffrey definitely made some cake. Those were just some of the ones I remembered through the copious Claret we also consumed as an integral part of the night's event does make the memory distinctly flawed.

We had almost reached the end of the year when the talk I was secretly most excited about arrived. It was given by a wonderful young man called Henry Starling, a quiet and thoughtful type of lad with such a bright and brilliant mind. He teaches Yeats at Stanford now I believe, a truly marvellous brain. What I quite clearly remember was his soft, southern voice never raising itself to an impassioned roar or excited bellow, like some of the others had. He was calm and steady, impressively unwavering in his delivery of speech.

I of course cannot recall every part of his speech, and am not sure that would be allowed under the covenant of our secret society code but I do remember this part...

'Mathematicians can talk us through the Fibonacci code of nature, prime figures and encryptions that respond to millions of the earth's natural sequences but are unable to tell us which exact number makes up a family.

Geologists can lead us over every square inch across every Continent and Ocean yet have not the capacity to explain to us the actual place where we feel is our Home.

Medics have repeatedly proven to us all in microscopic detail how the human heart is shaped, it's vital significance and how it relentlessly pumps to enable our bodies to remain, gratefully, alive but they cannot show us in physical, practical or visual terms where Love is created or stored.

Why has Poetry continued to exist over and through the centuries since the beginning of time? How does Poetry remain when to conclude from all of your discussions this past year, there is no rationale for it? No practical place. No reason to ever have continued.

There is no truly good world we would live in where Poetry does not exist. It is through Poetry that we are defined as original yet connected spirits. What I am referring to is the loving, furtive poems that distil and extract the very inner truths about us. Neruda, Bukowski, Cummings, Shelley, Browning. Using bare simplicity, enhancing each deliberate chosen word, punctuation , page spacing, creating the immediacy of an intimate offering, of some private confession.

'… Find what you love and let it kill you.

Let it drain you of your all. Let it cling

onto your back and weigh you down

into eventual nothingness. Let it kill

you and let it devour your remains…'

For some, Erhmann, Kipling, Shakespeare compose almost step by step guides to explain life and the multitude of obstacles will face and ideally overcome. Many of these hold whole lists of valid answers to our emotional landscape and place in it. Why wonder when you can share from the voices of past others who've discovered these secrets already?

Poems are the absolute astral core of us; built from our own uncharted nucleus, and this is where we will find the clear truth about ourselves. Real Poems can never be formulated or manufactured or artificially conspired. The truth and beauty that is reduced into poetic form can only be from whatever it is in the human being that exists nowhere else, by no one else. In gloried theory it perhaps can be seen to have little if any use to the heavily industrialised and wider modern working world but in practice…Oh my word, oh my, it elevates and it inspires and it burns and it bleeds, it cries and it relieves suffering we did not even knew existed within us. We read poetry to know the world on that mysterious soulful level. We write poetry to expel parts of us that need to find a voice that only other souls can hear.

For me, our World's secret is Poetry. The only proof we have that souls exist and we each are one of them. The word Soul is cited much over centuries, across every culture that its original essence can be both conflicting and commercialised, but I believe it is to this which I refer.

It means we matter. We are not just the breaths we take or the years we last. Our resonated glory does not depend on our financial wealth or our working status but on how we as people understand the very human connections that poetry exalts; Passion, Loss, Devotion, Humour, Joy, Destination, Anguish, Fear, Affection and Love; most of all, and never more so than Love. It is a small word that absorbs us all, built from the very reason we are created.

To exist you require a Body, to Love you require a Soul, to understand Souls we created Poetry.

Cummings writes;

"here is the deepest secret nobody knows

(here is the root of the root and the bud of the bud

and the sky of the sky of a tree called life; which grows

higher than the soul can hope or mind can hide)

and this is the wonder that's keeping the stars apart

I carry your heart I carry it in my heart…"

So here is my challenge to you. What is it that speaks directly to you, what matters most above and beyond the trivialities of day to day? What poem, already written, is an absolute reflection of your celestial soul? Because when you do find it, you will, for perhaps the very first and only time, discover who you actually are and what your time on this planet can truly be worth.

"I am a child of the universe no less than the trees and the stars; I have a right to be here. And whether or not it is clear to me, I am in no doubt the universe is unfolding as it should…Whatever my labours and aspirations, in the confusion of life, I shall keep peace with my soul."

And this revelation will be your solace, your absolution and your brutal singular truth from which you will then be able to live your lives full unto the magnificent depths it was meant for."

We all sat transfixed in a reverential hush. That didn't ever happen, I surely remember that part. The group took a minute or so to think in the silence. A moment passed before Andrew stood up, raising his glass. Ahmed, Juan, Richard, Geoffrey, Ishmar, every single other scholar there, including myself, picked up our glasses and lifted them to the direction of Henry, still stood, straight backed, upon the bench. Someone leant forward to pass him his own goblet filled with wine as he nodded in appreciation to Andrew first, then all around, before toasting, 'To Poetry and Souls!' 'To Poetry and Souls!' we happily responded, amongst the whooshing of liquid and the clinking of drinks.

And that evening was the beginning of our Aslan group appreciation and collecting of Poems together. We have continued this literary fascination and shared discoveries of new or forgotten verses to each other for almost three decades and counting, and I doubt we now shall ever stop. What it gave me was a lifelong love affair of this exquisite language and its power, and for this I have been eternally grateful.

Years later at an old masters evening I'd been invited back to, I discovered from talking to my old Classics Lecturer, Canon Reuben Darcy, that at our specific University every four years or so there would be a secret club formed to discuss exactly what we 'Aslan's' did. Often in the same hidden hall chosen for the identical reasons we had. In fact he himself had been in one, as had his mentor before him, and as far as he knew it had been occurring since the College first began. We were hardly the original revolutionaries we had presumed ourselves to be.

I asked him, possibly too boldly as we were in fact referring to confidential results, if they had reached any worldly conclusions themselves. Good humouredly he sat pensive for a long while before a wide smile broke out upon his elderly Jurassic face, and his eyes lit up with cheerful recall. "Oh my dear boy, the wonders of youth. All those splendid unblemished, ingenious minds." His low clipped voice was very amused. "Yes, indeed, we reached our answer of course, that was the point of the club. We deigned ourselves to be very efficient I'm proud to say." He tapped his nose in happy mime. "Never reveal, my good man, to an outside member. I'd be quite rightly hauled across those infernal hot coals even now." To which I of course nodded in gentlemanly understanding, slightly disappointed though, I must admit.

Yet after the pre-drinks, hearty supper, entertaining anecdotes and post-dinner Brandys, as he got himself up many hours later to retire to his chambers, wined and dined now much relaxed with those plentiful golden spirits, the Canon leaned over and whispered to me as he waved his goodnight to the others. With a brief conspiratorial wink and a fondness of past recall that sparkled gleefully in his furrowed, veteran eyes, "All I will say though, young Edward, despite agreeing on the universal World secret answer we fellows in my club still couldn't decide on the honorary icon for it, though for me, Keats was always my favourite."

TO SLEEP

O soft embalmer of the still midnight,

Shutting with careful fingers and benign,

Our gloom pleased eyes, empower'd from the light

Enshaded in forgetful divine;

O soothest sleep if it so please thee close

In midst of this thine hymn my willing eyes

O wait the amen ere thy poppy throws

Around my bed its lulling charities

Then save me, or the passed day shall shine

Upon my pillow, breeding many woes

Save me from curious conscience that still lords,

In strength for darkness, burrowing like a mole

Turn the key deftly in the oiled wards

And seal the hushed casket of my soul.

John Keats

"A poet is a nightingale, who sits in darkness and sings to cheer its own solitude with sweet sounds."

Percy Bysshe Shelley

After

To: E. 'Boxland Boy' Cc: Re: Help

Hello Ed,

Well done you for asking for help. You've always been such an astute man, much wiser than I ever was. I wish I had more of that sense of human intuition. My own ragged life would have been a lot easier for me I'm sure. Very clever idea.

You know when Bertie died I was utterly bereft. Twelve years have passed now but impossible to get over. Every day I am reminded of him, the greatest love of my life, all I have lost. There are days I relish in it, the obsession of him and us. We are the star crossed lovers, the tragic doomed pair in all centuries of finest literature. We were the ones never able to be.

I know I've always been a miserable old sod so it seems fitting for it to have happened to me. I imagine that black dog of depression has forever been a welcomed friend of mine. The glass always half-empty as they say and yet more often than not filled with a very fine Malt.

Looking back I wish I had tendered my own grief up and into the capable hands of our wondrous Poets. So absorbed was I in hurting alone I never thought to out stretch into the library of loving books I have been collecting all my life. Funny what you can't see for looking. I suppose none of us can see clearly when sat in our own dark.

Well, I've chosen an American poet, not least for his similarity of spirits if not spirit. I don't wish to include a prose full of rainbow dreams and light at the tunnel's end bullshit. I want to choose one that connects with the absolute rawness of the love and loss. In my humble opinion it's wrong to present grief as anything else. Denial of this fact is tantamount to abuse and I just won't have it.

Staying with the US poets, I would have loved to have picked a cummings one, just for the pleasing fuck-off-ness of punctuation and grammar that would drive Geoffrey up the wall but for me there are too many of them that mean too much. I've bought you his compilation online today and have had it sent to your office so perhaps that counts as cheating. Never mind. You can add that sin onto my very long list, apparently us Buggers aren't going 'upstairs' anyway.

I hope you both come good from all of this. Christ knows I'm no emblem of mastered bereavement. It can be a real bastard of a world this one. Screws even the best of them, no idea why, but I do wish you both get over this hideous hurdle, make it through and find a way. And if you ever do, you might even find a minute to share it with me. I'm still stuck in the dark of it, a dozen years and counting, but perhaps that's for the best. This dark is where Bertie is, so maybe I'm just fine with it.

Your friend,

Andrew

"In the total darkness, poetry is still there, and it is there for you."
Abbas Kiarostami

Consummation of Grief – Charles Bukowski

I even hear the mountains

the way they laugh

up and down the blue slides

and down the water

the fish cry

and the water

is their tears

I listen to the water

on nights I drank away

and the sadness becomes so great

I hear it in my clock

it becomes knobs upon my dresser

it becomes paper on the floor

it becomes a shoehorn

a laundry ticket

it becomes

cigarette smoke

climbing a chapel of dark vines…

it matters little

very little love is not so bad

or very little life

what counts

is waiting on the walls

I was born for this

I was born to hustle roses down the avenues of the dead.

Chapter Twenty-Nine

"Spiteful words can hurt your feelings but silence breaks your heart."
C S. Lewis

After

It had been three weeks since Ed had begun his nightly poetry readings. He had started with his favourite Auden copy, choosing one poem a day. It had been met as feared, with no recognition or applause; no sudden burst of affection. Not even a simple turn round of her magnificent head. The beautiful arch of Izzy's spine fell in parallel with the long chair she had now chosen as her preferred seated spot. A fine knitted grey cardigan draped from her shoulders and tucked over her folded knees. The delicate white soles of her feet poked out towards him, clean and fresh as if they'd never been walked on.

Her back view now more familiar to Ed than any other, remained steadfastly in his sightline as he settled himself on the sofa across from her, and looked at the small pile of poetry books he had chosen from his office shelves. At the end of work he had placed them securely in between the four manuscripts he was already bringing home, tucking them in safe like smuggled treasure.

From the outside looking in, for those twenty-one days nothing had changed. She was still distant and enveloped in her silent world, lying down, staring out of the window. He, returning home, would walk in the room to find her, leave his satchel by the coffee table then walk through to the kitchen and prepare them dinner. Often something easy or handheld was required, risotto, a toasted sandwich, soup, small pitta chips. The little table beside her was a makeshift dining space.

Most days he would pull up a chair close to her and pass her morsels of food, the same way he watched as a young boy, his father do to his elderly and infirm Grandmother on their Sunday visits to her care home. It used to frighten him seeing somebody so old and wasted away, once blithe features broken and distorted, arms and legs not working, unable to even lift a spoon or fork to sustain some quality of life. And yet here, in the prime of younger years, he was doing the same nurture, haunted by the same incapacity of self-care by a loved one; worrying that it would never get better, that it would always be this, or even get worse.

Once he read the chosen poem of the evening, Ed would scribe it down onto a blank sheet of cream heavyweight paper that they kept in the small oak bureau used for correspondence. His strong hand gripping the elegant ink pen firmly, its spider black cartridge clipped in, as he wrote with perfect loops and swirls across the pale paper with striking results.

The poem's title would be written at the top, using mostly capital letter for the initial words. He would not underline it or even add the poet's name until the end. Firstly he wanted to give value for them outright, he very much wanted the words and phrases to ebb and flow, be original and matter for their own sake, not heard with any underlying assumptions by the reader from seeing who composed it first. This last bit was also partly a tease, an element of intellectual fun for Izzy, giving her a chance to guess who had written each before checking the end for the answer.

Many she would recognise instantly, some he thought, she'd never seen. A few she could hate with their grating style or arrogant statements on issues important to her. A number she could feel deeply moved by as each line or intention touched her own adored feelings like a harmony of mirrored wishes. A couple of them could be so far off the mark from her own state of mind that they leave her indifferent, immaterial to that moment and easily forgotten. Whichever reaction she would have he simply wanted her to have one.

Tonight he had chosen "If I Could Tell You" by his beloved Auden. This he recalled being one of her favourites too. The same poem she had quoted to him on their second date, in a dark corner of a hotel bar after an afternoon walking around the glorious Ashmolean Museum. A piece she knew by heart but left him to say the very last line. Something after that first time, they would often do. It was during that cup of coffee, those perfect verses spoken, hearing her profound and heartfelt interpretation of the poem's meaning, was the very moment he realised he had fallen in love with her. She talked of how frightening Lions, Brooks and Soldiers leaving would actually be and how she longed for someone to be close enough to tell her in those fearful times, however hard; a bravery wanted, a truthful promise from one to another made.

At their coffee table that evening, once Ed finished scribing the poem, waiting a few moments for the ink to dry, he placed the paper into the grey bowl, his small act of defiance. He was claiming back this item of beauty made elegantly by a talented potter for the intention of beauty and admiration.

The day they chose it was as vivid to him as if it happened that morning. The two of them in love and in hope; the way he always wished them to be. He wanted this ceramic piece to salvage the importance of their happiness it once represented.

Ed reached down to the bottom of the bowl to place the hearing aids on top of the twenty sheets, stacked together looking like the beginning chapters of old manuscripts he would be given to read at the start of his career. Not too many typewriters or printers used back then. Those stories were immaculately inscribed on A4 white paper with all sorts of writing implements and hand styles. Mostly they were legible, thankfully. He always   . enjoyed the parts where the exciting action or high emotion would occur and each author tended to speed up the wording, pressing down harder on to the page, reflecting their passion and excitement of the upcoming plot. He'd imagine the pens racing across the page whilst their hand tried to catch up with the sprinting of their brain. He felt this was a privilege to see. Spelling mistakes, ink splodges, finger marks all present which gave an intimacy to the person lucky enough to be shown these pieces of personal creativity. Wine stains, coffee rings even tear drops all rested onto the pages of these works, unable to disassociate themselves from the author's own experience and real existence.

Ed's fingers clasped one of the plastic buds which he held carefully in his large steady hand as the other felt around underneath for its pair. His thought of leaving them both of the aids on the top of the pile in the bowl was not simply to hold down the papers but to place them encouragingly above them in case Izzy wanted to put them in and hear her read them to herself; in the daytime, when he was out and her world was private again.

It was awkward with the pages on top. He couldn't seem to touch the bottom so he lifted them out to get a clearer grip. Ed tutted to himself as he placed the sheets on the table beside the bowl, carefully keeping hold of the plastic bud for her left ear as he searched for the matching right. Had he knocked it off when removing the papers? He looked underneath the bends of the dish, lifting it up at check, but nothing. The abandoned autobiographies, the waiting poetry collections, the unread manuscripts, the glass of good red wine he had poured himself to enjoy whilst reading the new stories from work, were all on the table alone. There was no sign of it on the rug beneath and he stood up very gently in case it had flipped somehow onto his lap in all him inelegant moving, but still nothing. Where could it be? Had it fallen under the couch? Could he damage it if he moved too much to find it, trod on it or leant on it somehow? How easy was it to replace then? How would that even be possible without her permission?

Before Ed's panic continued rising, he stopped. A thought came, a brief possibility which seemed too remarkable to at first consider. He swallowed very slowly, his eyes resting on the empty bowl, his right hand felt hot with the tiny pearl of the singular hearing aid held safe within it. The room was still and somehow quieter than it had ever been to him as he heard the drum of his own heartbeat loudly beating. He dared himself to look up, to look over at Izzy. The back of her head was resting on the pale pink cushion. Ed could see her big, green eyes through the glass reflection looking up out through the window to the darkening sky. Her wavy brown hair falling off those thin, small shoulders save a little curl behind Izzy's right ear, sitting on the fold of her woollen cardigan, twisted back up the curl touching the bottom of her lobe. The lobe that was pushed down a fraction of a millimetre more than normal, than it was yesterday and the many days before: Changed due to the slight pull from the little plastic aid, neatly tucked into the top of the ear canal, kept safe there tonight, all this time so she could hear his new poem.

In the corner of the room, out of sight the glass bird tilted its fragile head to the couple in the room, entranced with this new state of play. It perched high on the ceiling, held fast on that wire with a view of those below. It was not listening to the gentle man's heartbeat that drummed powerfully around his body with elation. It was not listening to the soft whooshing and oooos breaths of the soft, sad lady on her long chair, letting those just-spoken, familiar poetic lines settle down from her listening to her mind and drifting on lower, soothing an ache that hid away deep, far inside her.

The bird was listening to the silent spaces. It was hearing all those fascinating parts in between the words out loud. It waited for what they would do next, waiting, waiting. It was trying to hold on for them. Its glass was light but the grief it held was heavy and the wire wasn't as strong as it was once before. It didn't want to fall and break, it really didn't, but what could it do apart from hold on and hope. Hope and hold on.

"I think it comes from really liking literary forms. Poetry is very beautiful, but the space on the page can be as affecting as where the text is. Like when Miles Davis doesn't play, it has a poignancy to it."

Jim Jarmusch

Time will say nothing but I told you so,

Time only knows the price we have to pay;

If I could tell you I would let you know.

If we should weep when clowns put on their show,

If we should stumble when magicians play,

Time will say nothing but I told you so.

There are no fortunes to be told, although,

Because I love you more than I can say,

If I could tell you I would let you know.

The winds must come from somewhere when they blow,

There must be reasons why the leaves decay;

Time will say nothing but I told you so.

Perhaps the roses really want to grow,

The vision seriously intends to stay;

If I could tell you I would let you know.

Suppose the lions all get up and go,

And the brooks and soldiers run away;

Will time say nothing but I told you so?

If I could tell you I would let you know.

If I Could Tell You. W.H.Auden

Chapter Thirty

"Reality only illuminates itself when it is illuminated by a ray of poetry."

Georges Braque

After

The Costas Family

Headington Hall, Oxon

Hello Edward,

I hope this note finds you well. I'm sorry I have not been able to be of more use to lovely Isobel in her time of crisis. I didn't want to force myself upon her. She's always seemed such a gentle thing. I don't know her well enough really to push my way in and offer verbal comfort or even be of much practical help, apart from the food parcels of course. Am happy to continue these on our weekly basis if you are? Please let me know if there's something you've had enough of or maybe would like me to include, I am very open to suggestions. Juan as you might recall from student days, is an absolute horse, there is nothing he doesn't eat and is beside himself with gratitude at even the most boring dinner. It's a complete joy to feed him but I don't expect all others to be so easily pleased.

Anyway I thought I might continue with my little posted messages to Isobel, if you were happy I go ahead. They're just small comments really, little thoughts or something light and kind that she might appreciate. There's no pressure on her to respond, they're all quite rhetoric. It's there to show her we're still thinking of her that's all.

When Juan told me how you were planning to help Isobel I was so impressed. I include a poem for her. Again, I hope you don't mind. Juan read me this in its original Spanish after my sister died ten years ago in a car accident. I didn't know the language well enough to translate it at the time but with his reading of it out loud to me, in a private moment of my mourning, I could feel the purpose of the poem and took enormous comfort in it. Its beauty has stayed with me all these years. I have a translation printed on a small sheet I use as a bookmark but actually I think when I recall it best, it is always in its primary language and heard rather than read. I don't think I ever felt more in love with Juan than when he did that.

I'm not sure if he ever said but Juan used to write me poetry when we were first married. Books and books of it, some were quite the epic sagas. I had forgotten about them until we spoke about your email the other day and I went to find them and there they were, safely stored in our hallway bookshelf. His rushed spiky sketches of Cupid and Eros scratched onto the covers. Well, we sat for hours reading and rereading them, to ourselves, to each other. It was the most wonderful evening we've had in many years. We felt sad we had lost touch with what was once so important to us. That earnest romance and early yearnings, so easy to gush and describe in flourishing verses but as I sit with him here, so many years later, that first flush of youthful excitement and adoring innocence long behind us, I wonder perhaps if it isn't really this time now when we should remark on true love and the honour of marriage. It is easy to sail in still waters, any two people can do that, but when tempests come and pass and we have weathered those storm, then that should be the part most celebrated. That to me is the creation and the earning of a much greater love.

I include my chosen poem below. I do hope you can read my writing. Juan always teases that I could put old Doctors prescriptions scrawl to shame.

Please know you are in our prayers. We wish you the best with it all. See you soon,

Cathy

"My role in society, or any artist or poet's role, is to try and express what we all feel. Not to tell people how to feel. Not as a preacher, not as a leader, but as a reflection of us all."

John Lennon

Shinto

When sorrow lays us low

for a second we are saved

by humble windfalls

of mindfulness or memory:

the taste of a fruit, the taste of water,

that face given back to us by a dream,

the first jasmine of November,

the endless yearning of the compass,

a book we thought was lost,

the throb of a hexameter,

the slight key that opens a house to us,

the smell of a library, or of sandalwood,

the former name of a street,

the colours of a map,

an unforeseen etymology,

the smoothness of a filed fingernail,

the date we were looking for,

the twelve dark bell-strokes, tolling as we count,

a sudden physical pain.

Shinto

Cuando nos anonada desdicha

durante un segundo nos salvan

las aventuras infimas

de la atencion o de la memoria:

el sabor de una fruta, el sabor del agua,

esa cara que un sueno nos devuelve,

los primeros jazmines de noviembre,

el anhelo infinito de la brujula,

un libro que creiamos perdido,

el sulso de un hexametro,

la breve llave que no sabre una casa,

el olor de una biblioteca o del sandalo,

el nombre antique de una calle,

los colores de un mapa,

una etimologia imprevista,

la lisura de la una limada,

la fecha que buscabamos,

contar las doce campanadas oscuras,

un brusco dolor fisico.

Eight million Shinto deities

travel secretly through the earth.

Those modest gods touch us –

touch us and move on.

Ocho millones son las divinidades del Shinto

que viakan por la tierra secretas.

Esos modestos numenes nos tocan,

nos tocan y nos dejan.

Chapter Thirty-One

"But in reading great literature I become a thousand men, yet I remain myself."

An Experiment in Criticism, C.S. Lewis

Before

The Café was almost empty. Every seating of tables and chairs could be seen from the counter stand which Ed appreciated. From any of them he could sit down and see who was coming and going in to the Alice in Wonderland themed coffee shop, which is of course very useful when meeting someone you didn't know.

Across from him a man in his fifties with his Daily Telegraph newspaper was perched by the window, next to him two female Vicars talked animatedly about the Bodleian Library opening times. On a table behind his own was a coat and umbrella propped against one of the chairs but no-one attending it. No other women, no woman, no other customer at all.

Ed's delayed train from London meant he was fifteen minutes behind and he detested being late of any sort. The respectful manners and discipline his schooling had instilled meant this tardiness irritated him. He was anxious on arrival that he had kept this Ms Bannister waiting longer than polite, as well as concerned by the knock on effect it would have on the 12.20 return train journey and the rest of his very busy schedule that day.

There were important meetings in the afternoon, firstly with Carron regarding their clients Christmas short stories compilations, as was fashionable that year, to make up as stocking fillers or the horrendously labelled 'Man Gifts'. Then Paul had organised a presentation on the sales figures from illustrated picture books. The new target markets and what specific subjects the Secretary for Education had kindly revealed to him, as to what they were looking for to be included within the curriculum next. A real jewel of knowledge ahead of their competitors which only cost Ed a very long lunch with a variety of fine wines sampled and consumed alongside the promise of two newly printed limited editions of The Hobbit his company was producing, being hand delivered to the Secretary's children the day of release.

As Ed ordered his second plain black filtered coffee from the bored student working at the till he wondered for the umpteenth time that day why on earth had he bothered to agree to this meeting so efficiently organised by Paul, liaising as he so helpfully did between the two of them. Ed hadn't even met this Isobel or communicated to her in any way since replying his thanks and confirmation of attendance to the up-coming Festival evening. It was Paul who had suggested a preceding meet so as to discuss more about this new event as its theory and intentions were indeed those very similar to Ed's own hopes for the Literature Industry and Britain's widened readership. Perhaps Fallon House could contribute more than just Ed's presence. Perhaps there was a correlation of intention that could promote some sort of partnership of ideals. It could help them promote their authors as well and serve as a voluntary goodwill-ness of raising awareness and increasing numbers for their iconic trade.

From getting off from the station, walking the brief minutes up Park Street, through Beaumont passed the Playhouse, up to the café at the opening of Broad Street what Ed did feel absolutely sure of was that this Isobel, whoever she was, was indeed right. If a Book Festival should be started anywhere in the country, or to his mind, world, it was here in his own Oxford such was his loyalty and love of the place. He admitted the visit to his old university roots was a pull as he hadn't travelled this way for longer than he cared to think about, and this small trip reminded him just how much he loved it. The haunting spires tall enough it seemed, to touch clouds, the beautiful architecture of the college buildings hemming in the city centre with a protective and authorative encasement like a wisely tutor gathering up his waiting class. A breathing, vibrant centre full of people of all ages, stages, colours and creeds, reading, reading, reading: Noses deep and minds lost in old blistered-spine paperbacks, chubby infant palms stickily gripping brightly painted board books, slender, careful holdings of the ever fragile comic or the *Graphic Novel* to those older than teenagers purchasing them, glossy new hardbacks chosen straight out of window displays, destination maps of wanted sightings, photocopied research papers anxiously prepared, up and coming bands gig times on coloured paper flyers, small restaurant menus of favourite specials, all being absorbed and revelled in by these urban wanderers. The various typefaces and print dents. Each infinitely handsome and delightfully different like miscellaneous stars in the constellated night sky. Yes, this was absolutely his heart's home. How could he not support such a place and on behalf of the very thing he enjoyed the most.

Taking his hot drink and settling himself at the wooden table with the clear view of the gated entrance to Exeter College opposite, his ears pricked up with the banging of indoor doors and clattering of dropped hard things on the cold tiled floors.

"Oh I'm so sorry. Oh dear, what I mess I have got myself into. Thank you so very much. Oh dear…" and more muttering of the same was coming from the corner of the café where it indicated Toilets and Staff Only.

Ed glanced over to see what the noise was about and noticed two adult women of opposite ages coming through the doorway together. One elderly, possibly in her eighties, her grey hair tied back badly like the attempt of a little child. She wore her lilac sweatshirt weathered and past best over her old-person-trousers, or 'slacks' as they so enjoyed naming. A trouser type having been purchased from an actual shop somewhere, who knows where, but only those above sixty-five seem to be invited in this secret store: It had the privacy of a priest hole. Items in it were unsaleable to the youths, never even appearing on the hangers in charity shops that were popping up on the high streets in ever more frequency; a holy grail of rail. This grandmother-esque lady was gratefully holding on to the younger's arm with both her thin, frail hands, smiling brightly towards her as they walked to the quiet table in the corner.

"Please, that's quite alright. It's no trouble at all. Now are you well enough to sit here for a moment whilst I go over to get you a nice cup of tea?" the girl in her twenties was asking. She was faced away from Ed now addressing her elder. In the world of people watching he used to be quite the expert at, all Ed could decipher about her initially was that the young woman's clothes were elegant. She was wearing a long black skirt hiding under the ankles, some sensible but possibly trendy black pump shoes. Her pale grey woollen jumper looked soft and delicate, not too big to swamp her, not too fitted as to tighten around her but that perfect balance of just right cosy yet flattering. Her large colourful scarf she had wound around her neck, as far as this angle could see, was fun in its graphic design and quite striking in its manufacture. To the trained eye it would be recognisable as an original screen-printed and hand sewn piece of fabric made by a very talented artist, perhaps a scholar from one of the excellent local Art colleges nearby. To all others it was simply something very beautiful that she wore with graceful thought.

Twenty minutes late was on his watch and Ed sipped at his coffee as he continued feeling irritated at himself for such an unusual effort made for a complete stranger who didn't have the curtesy to turn up, in a place down the road from her own address.

He busied himself by taking a thin novella out of his jacket pocket. It was a small copy of Ted Hughes' The Iron Man. For many reasons Ed would find himself returning again and again to this astonishingly stark and haunting piece. The clarity of the poet's tone, the gentle pulse of the story's tension that rose steadily throughout the tale, the ultimate peak of battle between the two main characters caught his throat upon each read as he, despite knowing the victor, would persevere as if he did not yet know the outcome.

'...The Iron Man came to the top of the cliff. How far had he walked? Nobody knows. Where had he come from? Nobody knows. How was he made? Nobody knows..."

He was so caught up in the familiar starting lines that he did not hear the young lady's question at first ask. "Excuse me, I'm sorry to bother you but are you Mr Williams?"

The voice came from the young lady who had been helping the old woman before. She was facing him now and Ed could see the full features of her happy and hopeful face. Her large green eyes full of kindness and curiosity, her slight nose above her plump, smiling lips wrinkled a little as she noticed he had yet to reply. Her skin was the colour of caramel and just as immaculately smooth, matching faultlessly with her dark brown glossy hair she had caught up into a large metal grip, leaving a few strands down that she had tucked casually behind her ears. Ears that held something foreign in each of them he couldn't quite see. Her head slightly tilted as she leant in a little further in to repeat her question.

"I'm so sorry to trouble you but I'm waiting here for Mr Williams, only I got a bit waylaid with helping a woman who had taken a fall. I'm not sure what he looks like you see, I know that sounds terrible, quite unsafe." Her voice directed to him was soft but not quiet. She spoke with a confidence in her speech but no air of rudeness at all; a careful, sincere tone that Ed felt captivating.

"Yes, that's me. I'm Ed Williams." He got up from his seat in acknowledgement of his guest and outstretched his hand to shake hers. "My train was delayed, I'm very sorry I am late."

"A bit like him then." She said as she pointed to the painting of White Rabbit character looking at his pocket watch, in the frame behind her. They both laughed.

"Can I please get you a drink to try and make it up?" He asked as he gestured the counter behind them.

"Oh yes please, a cup of tea would be perfect. Thank you. I'll just move my things." She walked over to the empty table which had the coat and umbrella. Looking towards the old woman as she did so, checking to see if she was better and in no further need of assistance, she smiled sweetly at her.

The knot of annoyance that had been sitting in Ed's chest before had eased immediately and instead of going away entirely it had been replaced by another sensation. One he had a familiar feeling of but couldn't correctly place. It was equally a warmth and a chill. It held in it a small lump of something unknown, a spark of potential; the churn of new possibilities both within and outside of his control.

That same fuse that had been lit upon first reading her letter remained, burning brighter now with this real life introduction and with it a fierce sense of responsibility for the now. How he behaved on this their very first meeting would be remembered by them both forever. What words he spoke and their intentions, his posture, his movements, his whole balance of behaviour would be interpreted by this new, most delightful woman and it over-took him entirely. He so desperately wanted her to like him, to be impressed by him. He hoped she would be in life the way he had read her words that very first time all those weeks ago. He wished she remained as gentle and as thoughtful as he had earlier observed with helping that elderly woman before. He so much wanted to know all he could about her immediately and excitedly, without seeming too keen or too over bearing.

Ed watched as he stood at the counter. Izzy sat down in the chair opposite his glancing at the front cover illustration of Hughes book he had left there. Her eyes studied it keenly, its rough, brick orange background that contrasted harshly with the heavy charcoal ink brush sweepings framing a matte, tin blue giant, facing away from the viewer. The drawing's eyes blunt white light streaming away to somewhere further than the vignette size allowed, his strong metal feet marching defiantly away, following that curious glowing beam.

The waiter pushed the cup of English breakfast tea towards him on the counter as Ed paid distractedly, too much as it happened, without ever looking away from Izzy. He stood feeling the same as he did here in Oxford all those years ago, a shy, naive young man untrained and helpless in the ways of charming women. He was lost in how he could recover this situation to being something more than a simple meeting, a work chat. That anxious knot of perfect intention within him refused to go away.

Ed took a few more seconds to study as Izzy touched the cover of his copy of Ted Hughes' book so softly as if it was as fragile as a cat's ear. Her eyes wide with thoughts of the joy that this classic novel provoked in her, slightly misted with her own remembrance of reading. A small smile reaching upwards from her generous lips as she blinked slowly recalling holding her own version many years ago, its crisp sturdy pages printed with a combination of both letters and pictures, sharing in their own talents of telling the fabled story. The scent of steel blades on the edges of those immaculately cut papers, the faint tang of the glue used to bind them together at its central base and the new lacquer used to seal and laminate the stronger outside cover, its deliberate designed colours and typography enticing the reader as to what treasures could be found waiting inside. All this culminated in an invisible fog of happiness around her, a true state of imperceptible human bliss only recognisable by a fellow addict. It was this response, so akin to his very own on the subject he loved most, that he was both thrilled and relieved in equal measure.

Ed now felt a possible sense of confidence occur. He took the filled blue and white patterned china cup over to their table and sat down across from her, ready to begin. He had a whole library of books, stories, poems, proses, quotes, plays and more held safe within him that he would now be able to share, page by page, with the young woman he was so enchanted by. Nervous yet hopeful, he began.

The elderly lady sat alone in the corner table who Izzy had so kindly helped earlier had been watching the scene quietly. Her old yet astute eyes that had witnessed so much over her many years saw the careful and minute exchanges between these two strangers, first slightly stiff with initial caution and then as moments progressed a lightness filled those spaces. It was as fluid and as natural as a song: The way their faces happily responded to one another, the way their shoulders leant further forwards, their necks angled with careful listening, her easy laugh from his interesting literary observations or borrowed author lines to fuse them further together.

The old woman stayed, much longer than she had planned to that morning in the café, staying and just sitting, watching, listening, lifted in her own spirits at the privilege of witnessing the very start of a brand new and exciting love story, never able to see them again, never able to know what the outcome or future chances would be. The act of simply seeing the start of something so innocently precious was good enough for her.

The framed picture above her from Lewis Carroll's iconic work simply read, "I knew who I was this morning, but I've changed a few times since then" and the wise woman smiled knowingly in agreement.

A while later, for the first time in his life Ed phoned ahead to the office to cancel and redirect all of his other meetings for that day. And in a way he never left that table, that day, that woman.

Had she ever known, that old lady would have been delighted.

"The only calibration that counts is how much heart people invest, how much they ignore their fears of being hurt or caught out or humiliated. And the only thing people regret is that they didn't live boldly enough, that they didn't invest enough heart, didn't love enough. Nothing else really counts at all."

Ted Hughes, *Letters*

Chapter Thirty-Two

"Aren't all these notes the senseless writings of a man who won't accept the fact that there's nothing we can do except suffer it?"

A Grief Observed, C. S. Lewis

After

Thursday 4/6 - 5.30pm

They sat together in Carron's office corner, that wonderful space. Tonight it successfully imbued that small sanctuary feel, with its familiar and comfortable furnishings, its pleasing temperature of warmth emitting out from the old, rusted radiator that served the historic building over decades like a pre-loved toy tin soldier. Her choice of flocked wallpaper, her selected gold framed paintings, classic, elegant, gently enticing so as to render her seated guests into trustful pledges and future contracts, honoured confessions of work, struggles and whispers for help if need be.

Her job, in these chairs, was very much more than simply book readings and gathering client signatures for documentation. She needed to establish the exact balance of friend, parent, manager and therapist. As much as she came across smiling, wide eyed with intelligent empathy, behind this was an incredibly shrewd and savvy businesswoman determined to be part of a literary empire making itself respected and renowned over all the big cities throughout the world; an empire that her son-less father would have been quietly proud about.

The first completely unplanned Thursday that Ed joined Carron after work began to take shape as a weekly event. There was no prior discussion of this, no talk, no new invite, but simply as the first time he placed his bag by her doorway and walked through, taking in hand the poured drink and settling into the leather armchair Ed felt able to relax and he welcomed those few hours he could sit and be out of charge, be the one taken care of for a change. It was their third Thursday post-work chatting that day, of getting back home later than the usual.

In office hours Ed was as diligent as ever. He was so distracted by the reading and the organising and the planning and the ever-changing interests in the publishing world that he didn't get the chance in those daily times to dwell on his home life. His office or meetings didn't attach themselves to moments of emotional waves or personal questioning they represented a solid, dependable place he could retreat to and indulge in everything he had been *before*.

If he had taken time to look further into this he would have noticed it was where for now he was happiest. His business within these four rented rooms inside this picturesque antique example of Victorian architecture was level and safe, vibrant with celebratory insights. Most importantly it felt alive. The buzz of creative forces, discussions of world views, descriptions of unchartered planets or fictitious creatures that roamed unidentified lands, sumptuously written Heroes or dreamily presented Queens, hardened political biographies or tales from newly chartered mountain treks made the encasement within these strong London walls his way of surviving.

Here he was, Edward Arundel Williams, Author and Publishing House founder, mentoring many a brilliant writer along their tenuous yet wondrous story paths. He was not a husband to a lost wife. He was not a father without a child. He needed these solid ramparts, those pale clay dependable bricks, the over painted wooden window frames, the cracked but polished red and black entrance tiles worn with over a century of crossings. He knew who he was here. He understood his role and could achieve his expectation of industry.

"The new book Arthur Valentine has written arrived Monday." Carron began. Her voice was soft, pensive. She was about to discuss something that was concerning her and tried to take a little breath to read the energy in the room. Her slight apprehension was indiscernible to Ed who had sat himself deeper into the chair's cushion, enjoying the soothing heated temperature in contrast to the sounds of the heavy spring rainfall hitting the pavement in the dark outside.

"Oh yes! I love that his last one, A Captain's Dust, did remarkably well both here and actually in Scandinavian sales for the first time. We've been waiting for this new one for a while now. It's been three years in the promise."

"Yes he does take his time it feels. Those books are all different but that's so much part of the beauty of them. That thin strand of recognition to bond them but nothing repeated. Time wise Eric Ward at least writes short stories in between his epics and Nancy Wardale fills the book gaps with her stage plays. Excellent last one at the Southbank Centre, 'Chasing Angels', did you manage to see it?"

"No unfortunately I didn't make it this year. Izzy always loved to go but…well, this time…Perhaps we'll see her next one." And with that subtle mention of her Ed took a large sip of his drink and insentiently sighed out loudly. Not realising Carron had been looking for clues, not expecting in this quiet and safe confine he was being checked for signals.

"Of course, completely understandable…" she murmured comfortingly, leaning over to fill his glass a little more. These weekly events had revealed the more amber spirits consumed the more relaxed Ed seemed to be. And the looser his tongue with private thoughts previously kept tightly inside between the hours of eight o'clock in the morning until five thirty.

"I am very much looking forward to reading Arthur's new work. He never lets us know what to expect does he. We were talking only a month or so ago and he let nothing slip about the content. I wonder what the pivotal predicament will be this time." Looking up at Carron, who he guessed had already finished it. She would have done so immediately, starting the moment it arrived on her desk, deposited by Paul on Monday morning. Ed did not stop to wonder why she had yet to pass it on to him. It was unusual but not remarkably so.

"Yes, well he has completed this particular piece but for the first time, as far as I know, been unable to finalise the ending." Her comment peaked Ed's attention into sitting up straighter. This was something he had not expected.

"Really, that is a first. Over the years he had expressed his wavering intentions between the protagonists but as far as I'm aware he felt those matters usually resolve themselves as he continued writing the plot. He is so driven by the actions of his characters in the midst of creating sometimes he admits even he doesn't know what they going to do until he reads it off his own computer screen."

They both shared a smile. Every author, if able to decipher their own ways of writing, was incomprehensibly different. No journey the same to its final scripted destination. Ed and Carron should know. They published a book on this very subject two years previously. A compilation of interviews recorded and noted by a retired admired Editor with over ninety writers of every genre contributing their own methods, habits, superstitions and idiosyncrasies.

"This new one apparently has got him quite twisted up and he has been generous enough to ask us for help with the deciding on which ending to choose." Carron surmised.

"Well, I suppose he is nearly seventy now, no real age in the writing world of course, Tolkein didn't publish Lord of the Rings until he was sixty-three and Arthur's had almost fifteen books out by then. All still in print too which is miraculous."

"And aren't we both thankful for that!" Carron chimed as they raised their glasses and laughed. They were both so fond of both the man and also for everything it meant to their company.

"Paul suggested I should put up a statue or some sort of portrait to him in the reception." Ed raised his eyebrow, a slight smile remained on his lips, lips warm with the expensive whiskey he was enjoying savouring in these quiet, grown-up moments. It tasted of freedom and of history. It tasted of trying to forget.

"Though I fear that sort of acknowledgement might cost us another five percent in fees." Sipping simultaneously they enjoyed this closeness, this ease of mutual thought.

Carron reached forward to put her glass down onto the small table between them. The light in this corner was low and gentle. Ed's face in the under-shadows looked thoughtful and soft. For a man in his late thirties he was very attractive, more so with his lines and slightly aging temples. The many years before when they first started Fallon, they were both determined twenty-somethings, full of enthusiasm and ambition for this inspiring industry. That obsession for the written word and all its guises had only grown stronger as the decade and more progressed. Their professional relationship had continued almost like siblings, sometimes twins; working together as a tight, trusted team, similar and familiar in direction and style. Ed filled out the Oxbridge community that still very much existed, strong discussions with alpha males, high intellects and old money, whilst Carron busied one business level beneath, the Authors, the Illustrators, the Agents, the Book Sellers: Equally valuable, both essential. The pair managed themselves like the flocks of black birds you watch in the skyline, dipping and weaving in automatic understanding, a telepathic choreography; that unsaid link.

The reading of the novels was something they promised from the start they would always continue. That 'slush pile' from postal delivery or printed out email chapters. There were occasions, quite rare but beautiful moments when a manuscript would come to them as an original piece of art, be that pen written, hand painted or sketched like a film story board within an anonymous seeming notebook. Whether it be short stories, an anthology of poetry, novella or books about the infinite subjects of this world and beyond, every single effort had been made by someone who felt it was worthy for it to be noted down and passed on to another. All gems of a sort, each from one person's time and commitment, a view inside a stranger's world and that privilege of shared private information like a priest's confessional or a best friend's promise. It remained Ed and Carron's favourite part.

As was the practice between them Carron would glance over each first and hand on to Ed with her initial notes. Certain authors, their most successful or personal choices, took precedence, and demanded more attention and dedication towards them from all Fallon's business' specified areas that would in the end complete the story's production. Andre Theirry was the best seller this year in Fiction, Margaret Orly their biggest across the foreign markets, Billy Hawthorne in the ever-expanding celebrity Cookery and Arthur Valentine was their oldest and most valuable client. The very first client Ed ever signed. A wise decision as it turned out, because it was the sales of his classic stories based on a variety of moral decisions from invented fated circumstances that the readers bought and read in their droves.

Valentine's work had not only been made so far into three films, two home British ones and one American cult movie but were regularly adapted into various BBC or additional TV dramas to include the latest up and coming actors, a sort of television theatrical rite of passage in the millennial times. Fallon Publishing ensured Arthur Valentine became the unquestionable success of the Literary World he rightly deserved, but it could also be said that Valentine made Fallon. Without Ed having taken a risk on his previously eight times-rejected manuscript by other more cautious Agents and Editors, it was possible that his business could have been overtaken or financially merged well before now.

Luckily, in reality it made both himself and Carron a lot of money, most of which was used to put back into itself so other writers could be seen and new stories to be told. Valentine's published works over the years had a huge impact on Ed's life satisfaction and hopeful possibilities.

Carron had indeed read Arthur's new work, *A Memory Made of Light*. It was lyrical and poignant. It was full of emotionally charged incidents and sensitive human trauma and like each of his other books, it linked in to the own lives of every reader, directly experienced or peripherally empathetic. This story would matter to them, no matter their age, culture, background or beliefs. He had managed to display a situation that would touch them all. That was his genius. His simplifying of any given situation and presenting it in such a way it could be played on any human heart string. Valentine was an emotive converter into the base of human condition, the commodity of Life language.

Except this time, this choice was something Carron wasn't sure they as colleagues were able to deal with. As much as she perhaps, needed to know the answer, the timing of this was fragile. Yet it was an essential, ultimately fearful wave raging brutally ahead towards them, this surge a long time coming, huge and suffocating. One she had no idea how to quell.

Yes Arthur Valentine was very important. What they didn't know, what they couldn't know was how his new and ultimately last novel would absolutely change the future for Ed, for Carron and for Izzy. How could they? The book hadn't been finished yet. He himself had yet to decide on an ending for it. It was a moral dilemma far closer to them all then any of them realised.

It would in fact, much later on, be Arthur's most celebrated work but it would be the choice of endings that would determine this so. It had to be right. It had to be completely the perfect answer. But this faultless choice would only work with two. Two people, not three. Mr Valentine was inadvertently going to change something between them all; now and forever.

The only thing for sure was that.

"Did you know dear, how much you took away when you left? You have stopped me even of my past, even of the things we never shared."

A Grief Observed, C. S. Lewis

Chapter Thirty-Three

"Part of misery is, so to speak, the misery's shadow or reflection: the fact you don't merely suffer but have to keep on thinking about the fact that you suffer. I not only live each endless day in grief, but live each day thinking about living each day in grief."

A Grief Observed, C. S. Lewis

After

It was a normal day of the week, Tuesday she thought. Her little ghost-girl was the image of a six month old baby. Her white towelling onesie with its pick snap buttons on the front was soft and cosy, allowing the small bundle, rosy cheeked and button-nosed, to lie beside Izzy as if asleep. Izzy dazed at the sight of her tiny chest moving up and down, just a fraction but perceptible, that little ribcage holding inside it such a wondrous beat, this remarkable sight of breaths taken which represented the very action of life itself.

However instead of staring at her daughter intensely and without change, inhaling all that maternal love, Izzy found her mind now wandering to another thought, a memory of time before.

There was a brunch menu, she was sure. The table was set with glasses of chilled orange juices and iced water, not red wine or their occasional Champagne. Izzy recalled the buff and red ticking striped tablecloths

They had listened to the radio that morning together as they sipped their coffees in unison, the mound of Saturday papers still to be finished, rested on the floor beside the sofa. The pile that would be doubled before the day was out with the purchase of that new days Sunday presses. Those repeated forty-eight hours stretched leisurely each weekend as they created the habit of taking different sections at differing times

Recently back from a weekend break in Paris, they returned with a new delight for breakfasting European style. It suited their enjoyment of leisurely meals, taking their time over eating, indulging in authentic and quality food. Izzy had not stopped smiling ever since. Their first year together had been the very best of her life and showed no sign of stopping. She was already planning the menu to cook him for their anniversary next week and the collection of new cookbooks they were increasingly pouring over and discussing eagerly together seemed to double every day.

Bob Dylan had been playing in the background as they had left for the local café which began the discussion as to the similarity or not of certain lyrics as poetry.

"It really depends on the song and lyricist I think." Ed replied as they walked hand in hand on that fresh sunny day down to the local café. "In that not all lyricists are poets and not all poems can be lyrics. They are designed for different purposes but perhaps, on occasions there is a crossover."

"Apparently Bob Dylan worked in a way that he would write snatches of lines and words then tear these into strips and make a form of collage out of them to create new pieces." Iz noted, recalling this from an article she had recently seen in one of the free Tube newspapers.

Nodding happily to this Ed replied, "it really is a great technique for working. I know of other Poets who use this. It's difficult sometimes with those wordsmiths so famous for having remembered or often quoted verses as it takes on a new meaning to whoever hears them. Dylan would often say that he never wanted to be a prophet or a saviour but it come from what others need at that time. I feel this is a lot like Poetry in that respect."

Ed and Izzy then spent the next four hours at the bistro table going back and forth on the subject and al it's interpreted possibilities. It turned out that Ed had a wealth of musical knowledge as yet undiscovered by Izzy, which she was thrilled to find out. Learning for her was a huge gladness, and as it was Ed, that exploration of his impressive and vast intellect only fuelled her love, and made these conversations feel like the best aphrodisiac. How she adored being charmed through her mind to her body.

On the radio station in the Café their Sunday playlist seemed to flawlessly match their conversation and as Ed expounded on the language and ideals of everyone he admired from Neil Young, Johnny Cash and Joni Mitchell to Lou Reed, David Bowie and Tom Waits. Iz sat in fascination and pure, deep joy.

"Of course there is someone whose work I love the most and he is considered one of the very best examples of how Poets and Musicians can create the perfection of both." Ed said. Izzy was intrigued. She knew too little about it to try and answer.

"Let's leave here now and walk over to the book shop round in the corner. I believe I saw a collection of his there and now I wished I bought it there and then. I hope it's not sold and I'll buy it for you. I'd really love to gift you his words." He said looking at Iz the only way she ever wanted to be looked at by him.

"That. Sounds. Wonderful." She replied, her small hand pressing each, singular word gently upon his skin in tender closeness.

Smiling now to herself Izzy wondered where that old volume could be. Perhaps she should get up and find it. Her mind was sluggish and foggier that before but she felt maybe if she looked, somewhere, here in the room…her bedside table? In the case by the dining room table? She couldn't think clearly…

The spirit-baby started crying from its imagined cot bed made from blankets on the floor beside her. Her tiny snuffled grunting and gentle moaning of need brought Izzy away from her remembering and into this daytime cause. She reached down and lifted up the small child, drawing in the floral, butter scent of her, holding her close against her breasts which appeased her daughter as they quietly cuddled, finding the warmth of each other.

For a moment Izzy felt that she had dreamed that brunch those months ago. That it was her husband who was the imagined family and it worried her that she didn't feel sure.

Time was running out but the more frightening part for Izzy was not knowing time for which one? The sound of the ticking timer that was pounding in her head made her breaths shallow and her hands shake. She rocked her beautiful baby to the rhythm of its noise to try and soothe them both. It was the countdown of an ending. It was a beat she recognised but didn't have the clarity of mind to place.

The bird watched the two below as they huddled together to gain comfort from the other but today it seemed unsatisfactory, that there was a crack that had now begun appearing in this day-dreaming like the large grey bowl on the table in that room. It stayed with them as they fitfully slept, chest on chest, rocking side to side to the timer's pace. The bird saw what she hadn't noticed. The bird knew that the timer beat to the precise speed of her own husband's heart.

"This is the only poem

I can read

I am the only one

can write it.

I didn't kill myself

when things went wrong

I didn't turn

to drugs or teaching

I tried to sleep

I learned to write

I learned to write

what might be read

on nights like this

by one like me."   Leonard Cohen

"Perhaps it has sometimes happened to you in a dream that someone says something which you don't understand but in the dreams it feels as if it had enormous meaning – either a terrifying one which turns the whole dream into a nightmare or else a lovely meaning too lovely to put into words, which makes the dream so beautiful that you remember it all your life and you are always wishing you could get into that dream..."

The Lion, The Witch and the Wardrobe, C.S. Lewis

After

BANNISTER BOOKS, Oxford

Est. 1867

Hello Ed,

I hope you are keeping well and not too busy with the Booker Prize finals that are coming up next month. It's a frenzy here at the store for the titles and I myself are trying to get them all finished so I can chose my own favourite before it's announced. Most years I do tend to agree or at least understand the reasons behind it. All except that awful winner in the nineties, you remember the one? We had huge heated debates at the long table over that I can tell you. Luckily the panel seemed to have clawed back respect since but some of us are still a little wary. Us literary folk have such elephantine memories so forgiveness in our precious pocket of the Book World can be very hard.

Anyway moving on, I enclose a copy of Isobel's medical files you requested, including the alternative institutions we consulted. I hope you find it helpful. I must also write that I'm so dreadfully sorry about this whole Isobel business and her regression. I feel I have passed her on to you with some sort of default trigger that you were not aware of when you married her. We believed so much that her past remained her past and had no idea it would or ever could come back so severely into this present. You must know that we completely understand if things don't change soon and she remains as she is, that you might need to move on with your life. We do see this as a possibility, one you would never choose outside of these circumstances.

Or perhaps you can think of it as a short break. Some much needed time apart to gather strength, a little relief and some perspective. She is always welcome back with us for however long it takes. This is not just a platitude, it is a genuine gesture. There is no time limit on this offer. Please take as long as you may need. We do not have to talk about this again but I write it here so you know this proposal is forever on the table.

Referring to your queries from your phone call earlier this week, from the shelves here in Izzy's old bedroom I found her copies of Greek Myths, Tolkien, Shakespeare plays but it was the seven Narnia books she spent most time with as I recall. Perfect age for them then of course, and you know how she is with her fierce loyalty of all things Oxford. I've included this box set too as they're hers anyway and you just can't tell what's helpful or not with these memory issues.

Later on she adored Fitzgerald, Didion and for absolute sure, all poetry. She was always welcome to help herself to the stock downstairs if she was careful with them so I'm afraid I have no idea which other books she read or not as she took then replaced them without question.

I spoke at great length to Marcel about your evening readings to her and we were both so touched at such an idea. When she was younger we did read stories to her at night before bedtime but never poetry. I think it's because I personally have always looked at poems (the ones I enjoy most) as being so intensely intimate, made for lovers to whisper confessions and divulge personal obsessive secrets. It's such a pleasurable adult experience to illuminate, uncover and disclose thoughts and profound emotions to another that I've only ever kept it within that framework. I know of many people who actually can't read poetry out loud because they feel it is simply too much, as if they are standing naked in front of crowds, the words in them so private and revealing, even though they were written by someone else, for someone else, sometimes even centuries before. I'm not (unfortunately at times) that self-conscious but I do know what they mean.

I imagine also for actors having to quote exceptional script lines of longing and devotion to one another, how it must be impossible to not always fall in love such is the power of our magnificent, emotive English language. I know there are certain Shakespearian speeches that would send me into an absolute hypnotic daze if they were quoted to me, one on one. Into the prosaic world of books there are infinite paragraphs I could class as the very definition of love and the heart-stopping, devastating effect it would have on the reader, both good and bad. Philip Pullman's character's words in 'Amber Spyglass' about eternity and atoms takes my breath away each time, without fail. Beautiful.

Anyway, I'll leave you here. Huge love to Iz. I'm including with this package a cashmere jumper I bought for her last week. I hope it fits and she will be comfortable in it. I cut out the labels inside as she always hated them against her skin as a child, I'm not sure about now. You would know best.

Right that all said, I will add my choice of poem for Izzy below. Marcel will provide his own. He is busy nose deep in the downstairs bookstore shelves as I write finding the *right one*. Thank you for asking us. These things really do feel quite a privilege to be involved in. We wish you the very best of luck.

Talk soon. Kindest regards,

Alex

"The secret of poetry is never explained – is always new. We have got no farther than mere wonder at the delicacy of the touch, and eternity it inherits. In every house a child that in mere play utters oracles and knows they are such. 'Tis as easy as breath. 'Tis like this gravity, which holds the Universe together, and none know what it is." Ralph Waldo Emerson

A Poet's Grief – Barry Middleton

Why must poets bleed

for the empty ache

of lost love, of lost youth,

the wickedness of death,

the dying pain of time,

and the agony of memories.

My tears are for the weight

of all unending grief,

for the silent inner war,

and for all brutality

of nations and of men.

I weep for the shame

the endurance of hate,

the frailty of caring.

It is a ripping knife

That tears a heart,

and kills the soul

with no saviour to redeem.

Planets whirl, moonbeams fall,

and evil creeps like a maniac

who stalks with hatred.

There is no answer,

the monster comes

hooded and red eyed

in the terrible night.

Speechless is my pain,

no tongue to speak the loss,

my love, my hope, my faith,

my peace, my soul, my life.

Marcel Romero, Jazz Pianist

Carino Mio Isobel,

Please forgive this rushed note. It took so long in finding the perfect poem to send for you that I am running behind so much. Alex is getting cross with me as he wanted this package sent days ago but I just couldn't do it until I found the absolute right one.

We have never talked too much about our parents, either of us. My own father was a cruel man, a big drinker and a loud bully. Once my mother died I think he struggled so much with the man I was becoming and my very liberal life choices that it was clear we would be estranged as I grew up and left my home behind. As I get older I feel sorry for a lot of what he went through, typical of my country's troubles at that time. It wasn't easy for any of them growing up under such a harsh and militant regime. And he as a single father maybe struggled more than most.

As beautiful a culture as it is, there was always an underlying shadow that felt all the good things, all the love and the life could be snatched away at any time. To some of us younger folk we embraced this as a freedom to celebrate the everyday as we never knew how long we would have. We would search for the most colourful, the most decadent and the brightest of everything. That was how we survived. To the elders they were more frightened. They closed in and shut off. It was easier not to love anything at all than have that love taken from them. I look back on them now with a sadness rather than anger. I wish I had known him in another way, before life beat him down and made him hard. A softer man, one without fear and a loss of hope in his coal black eyes, perhaps that man I could have made my peace with, perhaps he would have loved me whoever I became.

There was one night as a younger boy I do remember well, as clear to me as a full moon. It was just before I left. One of the last times I ever saw him. Coming home from my friend's house I stopped and watched him drinking on the veranda with his political buddies. It was the anniversary of my mother's death. She had been gone five years by then but he always remembered this date, above all others.

They all sat around discussing and cursing, swigging from old rum bottles and taking it in turns to point angrily towards the city lights or up at the sky to blame God or Fate or the Stars. He did not know I could see them, he probably would not have even cared. But amongst the arguing and the grumblings I watched as he stood up and quoted by heart this poem I share now with you.

He did not stop, he did not waver, his rendition of it was faultless and to everyone there that hot summer night, extremely moving. It was maybe the first time I thought my father had a heart, that somewhere inside of him, some place deep I had never seen was the ashes of a boy who did have longings and chances once long ago. And his eyes were bright and open to a world he was not in fear of or broken by.

I have been very lucky in my life settling here in this wonderful country, being accepted, finding a new family of my own. I wish you that same joy, the same harmony within your heart.

We love you so much our beautiful girl. Please find a way to come back to us. We miss you every day. Adios hija encantadora.

Marcel xxxxxxxxx

The Sad Mother – Gabriela Mistral

Sleep, sleep, my beloved

without worry, without fear,

although my soul does not sleep,

although I do not rest.

Sleep, sleep and in the night

may your whispers be softer

than a leaf of grass,

or the silken fleece of lambs.

May my flesh slumber in you,

my worry, my trembling.

In you may my eyes close

and my heart sleep.

Chapter Thirty-Five

"We can't have the happiness of yesterday without the pain of today…The pain then is part of the happiness now. That's the deal."

Shadowlands

I think it's sad that we can't re-read pages or chapters of our own lives like a favourite book. It would be so comforting to go back to the glorious times we've had and feel them all over again. Even the harder things, the scary or darker times would not be as awful because we now know what happens next and we can see how once we get passed them that there is often a better place ahead, made even more radiantly lit perhaps because of the darker parts before.

I want to read again and again that first day in the Café. That afternoon walking around the city spent in a haze of frenzied conversations and quotations on all our favourite works. The lines from a verse one would start and the other finish. The guessings of which novel begins with what sentence, or that ends with which striking phrase.

The laughing about famous fictional characters and their mishaps as we strolled along the river bank by the Castle, our fingers almost touching, are hands so near to holding. The wished-for kisses when the words were done.

I want to read again the first letter you wrote. Your strong, handsome handwriting explaining how much you enjoyed our meeting, how you hoped there would be many more. How it included a new book of The Iron Giant as you remembered I had left my own copy as a teenager, on a train. And it upset me so much to lose it because I adored it so, because my father had bought it for me and it was one of the few memories of him I ever shared to anyone and yet I told you after only hours of knowing you.

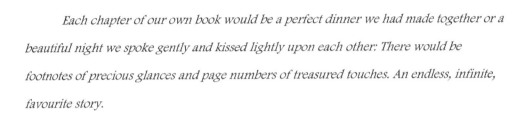

Each chapter of our own book would be a perfect dinner we had made together or a beautiful night we spoke gently and kissed lightly upon each other. There would be footnotes of precious glances and page numbers of treasured touches. An endless, infinite, favourite story.

Just. For. Us.

All. We. Were.

All.

We.

Are.   X

"A real book is not one that we read, but one that reads us."

W. H. Auden

Chapter Thirty-Six

"We were promised sufferings. They were part of the programme. We were even told, 'Blessed are they that mourn', and I accept it. I've got nothing that I haven't bargained for. Of course it's different when the thing happens to oneself, not to others and in reality, not imagination."

A Grief Observed, C. S. Lewis

After

cummings for Physical Love. Auden for Human Love. Neruda for Heart Love. Far too simple for him of course but there remained a truth in it.

Since the night he found Izzy awake with the rain, those moments of renewed gentle gestures and intimate space they shared, Ed very much wanted to indeed 'help' her as she asked him in that dark. The poetry readings had moved them forward he had hoped. There certainly felt a lightness in the evening air than before, a strand of possibility, however fragile and invisible.

Ed wanted to continue the evening poetry that he had chosen or been kindly sent by others. There were so many that meant so much to finding just one per day was almost too difficult to narrow down and he knew he shouldn't be too intense at the start. He sought to awaken her, to entice her.

Many times he felt this project was more for him than her, and he questioned himself for the hundredth time whether it was doing any good at all. What was the point? What did he even expect? Those nights when he finished writing the poem on the paper to put into the bowl, when his voice had finished filling the room and they were left with just that silence again, it could feel worse, it could feel like the verse's noise only highlighted the lack of one once completed. On those evenings he would place that sheet into the bowl as if he was a young boy begging for magic.

Drawing on events from some years before Ed managed to recall a morning they had enjoyed at the Randolph in Oxford. They had stayed together in his big, beautiful hotel room on one of his ever frequent trips up to visit Izzy. The walls were papered in a fantastical plush damask silk, the pale carpet underfoot was deep and luxurious and the bedding, where they spent a lot of their time wrapped up in or under, was starched white, the finest of Egyptian cotton and a thick billowing embroidered quilt, full of the colours of foreign peacocks and English spring lay folded at the foot of the bed.

The exciting and always innovative Playhouse Theatre was only meters away down the left of their window, and the imposingly brilliant Ashmolean Museum could be seen across the street. Its strong, domineering ionic columns that carried the entrance roof like a God's palace stood in front where they could see, each of the couple's joy lifted and enflamed at such iconic and dramatic settings; their city, their Oxford, that innate sense of home.

On such a day *before* Izzy had given him a book. This was not uncommon as they had begun from the very start sharing novels and volumes of work each time they were now together, to pass on thoughtful comments or wished offerings for the other's enjoyment and literary thrill. But this gift, her choice, was particularly special.

'100 Love Sonnets' by Pablo Neruda, the Nobel Laureate, was a Poet Ed had heard of, of course, and had read some of his more well-known pieces and yet he had never owned a compilation of his fuller works and thus he was delighted and intrigued in equal measure.

"Marcel introduced me to Neruda some years ago. With the joint South American connection and their mutual Spanish language he was a great admirer of the man, his strong politics and famed entertaining personality. He was certainly on Marcel's list of people he wished he had met." Izzy explained as they lay in the bed together, their breakfast on the trays beyond them almost untouched as they had a hunger of a different kind when meeting together again.

"I wanted them in both the Spanish and the English. I wanted without translation, to hear the exact choice of words Neruda had selected to express the very part of him he released. I then needed to hear it by someone who had taken great care in interpreting his voice and intentions, how somebody managed to know this poet's thoughts and voice and found it's matching other in our world of words and phrases. It was a wonder to me." Ed lay beside Izzy listening intently, his mind fully focussed on her telling, his hand absently stroking her own that rested between them, a soft touch of belonging.

"Yet Marcel could never read them to me and I didn't understand. He refused to speak them to me but simply gave me the book to read myself. I remember being angry. This was so unlike Marcel who was always so kind and obliging but he did not budge."

Izzy stared into Ed's eyes for a moment to register a flicker, a spark that he had guessed his own answer to the story. She smiled slowly; his beautiful brain, his perfect obsession.

"I know it now. I realise it today, here, with you." She slipped ever closer to him, tucking her head under his as Ed's arms pulled her against his warm, broad chest. The two pressed so tightly together as if they were indistinguishable, bonded as the same body.

"I love Neruda." She spoke into his neck, his hair bristling, his eyes closing. "His passion, his greatness, his adoration. How he describes worship, how he offers his soul to his lover. His answers about life and pity and duty discovered in amongst the very world around him. He knew of such great Love, he refused to live a life without it. And so…"

"Ummmm so…" Ed responded, as he gently kissed the top of her head, embracing the scent of her, the freshness so familiar to him. She raised herself up to meet his eyes again, her mouth too far away to reach with his own. She willed him to reply.

"I think you know why Marcel couldn't read them to me," she challenged, her smile widening. She had absolute faith Ed would be correct, such confidence that this loving man knew the very thing she did and more importantly, agreed with it. Ed breathed in hard, his smile opened to her, aware he was being tested, not minding at all.

"Of course he would not be able to. Works such as Neruda's can only be spoken from lover to lover. His lines are far too heart-felt, too affecting to be carelessly told. They are ways in to another, paths to each other that lead to the deepest, most tender part. No one should speak them to you except someone who is destined to awaken that inner most Love. It would be reckless to underestimate their power. Neruda's poetry can open something in us that can never be closed."

Izzy knew at that minute, that very second in time, that she had found the only man who she would fall in love with. He knew her as she knew herself, right into the very bones of her. He thought the things that meant the most to her and shone them back towards her in that they were more beautiful from his reflection. She was no longer alone. She was perhaps no longer unfixable.

"If ever you want to know how much I love you then I will read to you from him." Ed promised. "I am unable to write with his unmatchable genius, such divine talent, but if I could I would use those very same lines, the identical verses, it's as if he is *my* voice, that he is telling from my own core. Knowing him is the very best gift I could ever have been given. It's the only present I can offer you that means everything I believe in, in that I can offer you everything I am."

Iz watched him. His full mouth with its perfect sincerity, his brow furrowed in definition and Iz felt on the brink of a high cliff of emotion, a paradise edge and beneath her was a sea of foaming hopes and magnificent futures. She was teetering. She was breathless peering down, her heart stopped.

Lying there together he had picked up the new book she had given him and looked through in the quiet, to the one that touched him most that morning and he spoke, direct, clear like a solemn promise.

"I do not love you as if you were a salt-rose, or topaz,

or the arrow if carnations the fire shoots off.

I love you as certain dark things are to be loved,

in secret, between the shadow and the soul.

I love you as the plant that never blooms

but carries itself in the light of hidden flowers;

thanks to your love a certain solid fragrance

risen from the earth, lives darkly in my body.

I love you without knowing how, or when or from where.

I love you straightforwardly, without complexities or pride;

I do so because I know no other way of loving

than this; where *I* does not exist, nor *you*,

so close that your hand upon my chest is my hand,

so close that when I fall asleep it is your eyes that close."

And with the beginning of Ed's quotation of that poem she jumped, graceful and free, soaring down like a swooping bird, enveloping her whole body into that sea of elation, the steady water of Love, warm, ecstatic, pure Love.

Ed remembered the morning at the Randolph Hotel as keenly as if it happened that very morning. So cherished were those memories to him. There were days he felt he had to hold on to them or else lose her completely, all over again. A past between them that was better than their present.

He sat for a moment and thought. He had not spoken their Neruda since he began the poetry nights. It felt too much somehow, too loud. But the message remained the same for him, the promise. And it occurred to him from recalling something Juan's wife had mentioned in her letter that he could try something new, something so very private that Iz could perhaps find a space within her for it. Maybe this would be his 'help'.

It did not take Ed long to find the original book she had given him on the shelf beside the couch. He silently searched for the page, it was on thirty-eight and thirty-nine. The pastel paper ironed flat, the steely grey inked letters appearing proud upon the pale. It was many years ago since he had learnt what he needed now and he hoped she would forgive him such discrepancies and flaws. With a small cough and a shift in his seat, with a breeze of nerves that made his voice quiver only slightly, he slowly and carefully began.

"No te amo como si fueras rosa de sal, topacio

o flecha de claveles que propagan el fuego:

te amo como se aman ciertas cosas oscuras,

secretamente, entre la sombre y el alma.

Te amo como la planta que no Florence y lleva

dentro de si, escondida, la luz de aquellas flores,

y gracias a tu amor vive oscuro en mi cuerpo

el apertado aroma que ascendio de la tierra.

Te amo sin saber como, ni cuando, ni de donde,

te amo directamente sin problemas ni orgullo:

asi te amo porque no se amar de otra manera,

sino asi de este modo en que no soy ni eres,

tan cerca que tu mano sobre mi pecho es mia,

tan cerca que se cierran tus ojos con mi sueno."

Izzy turned to look at him. She knew each line he pronounced. She had heard it in her own head for a long time, a memory that had made. Her eyes were wide and grateful. Her green eyes wet and glistening with tears. Ed looked over when he had finished and saw her. The noiseless-ness felt important now. It felt an honoured space in which those words were carried across towards her, like the building of a bridge.

Izzy watched as he wrote the poem down with great care as he sensed her still looking. Once he placed the sheet in their bowl he gently walked over to her, his wife, and Ed reached his hand out, taking her lifted own, and with a new, warm, soft hush around them, he led her to their bedroom, simply to hold her for longer than ever.

Manuscripts. Left. Unread.

The bird resting above them was intrigued. It had seen a recognition between them of something it had not known. It was aware of a link they had remembered that had made their past come into their present time. It felt like the far away lighthouse shine seen from a lost ship. It felt like the first bud of a flower prospering from a plant long thought gone. It felt, dare it think it, like hope.

"And the verse falls to the soul like dew to pasture."

Pablo Neruda

Chapter Thirty-Seven

"For poems are not words, after all, but fires for the cold, ropes let down to the lost, something as necessary as bread in the pockets of the hungry."

Mary Oliver

After

Dear Edward,

Thank you for both of your recent emails, your first personal one enquiring after Elsie and the following group message. To begin I'll answer that Elsie is doing very well at the moment, thank you. The chemotherapy whilst taking a great toll on her energy levels and appetite (that they promise us will resume shortly), has shown a dramatic reduction in her tumour which they are now happy to operate and remove. This is an enormous relief, as you can imagine, and she's booked in to the Radcliffe next month.

The past five months have been fraught with uncertainty and fearing the worst but dare I write, at present we are feeling quite hopeful that this diagnosis is simply a part of a journey for her and not, as we had initially feared, the end of one. She remains in high spirits and her courage and determination, even on those harder days when she can barely lift her head off the pillow, seem full and boundless. I remain in awe and ever grateful of this and her.

Thank you both for your flower delivery as well as that yearly magazine subscription you chose and paid for. Elsie does indeed like that publication and has very much enjoyed reading its monthly editions. The short story competitions it includes at the back have delighted to the point of starting her scribbling in the ever present bedside notebook. This may indeed be the start of her next mystery novel. I wonder if I will guess the murderer correctly this time? Never managed to before so probably not.

My father always felt a little uneasy at a daughter-in-law so proficient in knowing multiple paths of execution. I always thought it was the reason he never wanted to stay over-night with us, not quite convinced he would perhaps wake up the following morning. He was certainly suspicious at with any food she may have been preparing, keeping an ever vigilant eye and taking his time once served at the dining table, to be sure someone tasted it first. Poison being the favoured choice of women killer's apparently. Ironic now she has been having such regular doses of it at the hospital in the plan to ensure her survival.

I was sorry to have missed the last Aslan meeting, it was just bad timing conflicting with Elsie's second round of treatments but I am very much looking forward to next year's. I wonder if Henry will be able to fly over for it again.

It's very hard to know what to write regarding Isobel as it is such a personal and in many ways, private grief. I would hate to suggest I understood, even facing what we have had to it seems as far apart as wind and water. No two difficult events are ever experienced in the same way. Is this a comfort or a flaw? I admit defeat to try and answer that and yet somehow your suggestion of looking to our Poet's shared words seems entirely correct.

With them I feel they offer no false empathy or light confession, revealing themselves with heroic truth in all passions. It remains the greatest gift to come across a poem that feels as close to your own state as if it had been written just for you. Good Poetry should indeed 'feel like remembering' and the right piece when discovered at the necessary time should feel, even as unique as your own life is, that you are not alone. It is that connectivity, that joining of voices across all time that resonates with another; someone they've never seen or met, shared the same country, history or even lived at the same century with, but a similarity of human sentiment strong enough to matter.

I would like to offer my selection on two parts. The first is the familiar piece by Dylan Thomas which I feel tackles the issue of the strength about Life around Death as beautifully as it possibly can. He manages to acknowledge the enormity of loss but maintains a thread of further possibility, an extension of surpassing it, which is a very thoughtful concept. When Ishmar played us the LP recording in his university room that evening many years ago now, of Richard Burton reading that same poem, slowly and expressively, like only his remarkable voice can, I was so moved by the experience I wept. Something about the glory of the exact, ideal words chosen, its heartfelt message combined with the thick, gravelled vocals spoken with such raw, emotive depth, spaced gently and carefully with an almost reverential solemn pace felt akin to a divine religious experience for me. Those moments in your life you are forever moved, a shift inside your head and yourself that remain sacred and unforgotten. I was so glad to have shared that with you all too.

My second would be a follow up from this. If Thomas is tackling Death then I wish to counter this with one with another Poet. I would normally perhaps go for balance and want to acknowledge the process and the circle, the Spring after Winter and if I may be so bold to say perhaps Hope after Loss but today that seems too large a concept to lay down. I wish to be gentle, choose something with a softer message. For this I include the great Marvel one. For me it remains one of the greatest love poems ever written. Telling a person you love them, requited or not, is an incredible thing to do. To be the recipient from someone professing such glory must, it must, be medicine for a broken soul. There are days when we can talk about the bigger things, the details, the dramas or the dreams, but it all comes back to Love in the end, doesn't it? Whether it is Thomas' desperation at his loss, losing a treasured one, heart broken, anguished and wishing for more time or Marvel's graciousness at future plans and attentive, earnest pleas, chances spent together, they both come back to the same: Always about Love.

Talk soon. In our thoughts,

Richard and Elsie xx

"Poetry is above all, a singing art of natural and magical connection because, though it is born out of one's personal solitude, it has the ability to reach out and touch in a humane and warmly illuminating way the solitude, even the loneliness, of others. That is why, to me, poetry is one of the most vital treasures that humanity possesses, it is a bridge between separated souls."

Brendan Kennelly

And Death Shall Have No Dominion – Dylan Thomas

And death shall have no dominion.

Dead men naked they shall be one

With the man in the wind and the west moon;

When their bones re picked clean and the clean bones gone,

They shall have stars at their elbow and foot;

Though they go mad they shall be sane,

Though they sink through the sea they shall rise again;

Though lovers be lost love shall not;

And death shall have no dominion.

And death shall have no dominion.

Under the windings of the sea

They lying long shall not die windily;

Twisting on racks when sinews give way,

Strapped to a wheel, yet they shall not break;

Faith in their hands, shall snap in two,

And the unicorn evils run them through;

Split all ends up they shan't crack;

And death shall have no dominion.

And death shall have no dominion.

No more may gulls cry at their ears

Or waves break loud on the seashores;

Where blew a flower may a flower no more

Lift its head to the blows of the rain;

Though they be mad and dead as nails,

Head of the characters hammer through daisies;

Break in the sun till the sun breaks down,

And death shall have no dominion.

To His Coy Mistress – Andrew Marvel

Had we but world enough, and time,

This coyness, Lady, were no crime

We would sit down and think which way

To walk and pass our long, love's day.

Thou by the Indian Ganges' side

Should'st rubies find: I by the tide

Of Humber would complain. I would

Love you ten years before the Flood,

And you should, if you please, refuse

Till the conversion of the Jews.

My vegetable love should grow

Vaster than empires, and more slow.

An hundred years should go to praise

Thine eyes and on the forehead gaze;

Two hundred to adore each breast,

But thirty thousand to the rest.

An age at least to every part,

And the last age should show your heart.

For, Lady, you deserve this state,

Nor would I love at a lower rate.

　But at my back I always hear

Time's winged chariot hurrying near;

And yonder all before us lie

Deserts of vast eternity.

Thy beauty shall no more be found,

Nor, in my marble vault, shall sound

My echoing song: then worms shall try

That long preserved virginity,

And your quaint honour turn to dust,

And into ashes all my lust.

The grave's a fine and private place,

But none, I think, do there embrace.

　Now therefore, while the youthful hue

Sits on thy skin like morning dew,

And while thy willing soul transpires

At every pore with instant fires,

Now let us sport us while we may,

And now, like amorous birds of prey,

Rather than at once our time devour

Than languish in his slow-chapt power.

Let us roll all our strength and all

Our sweetness up into one ball,

And tear our pleasures with rough strife

Through the iron gates of life:

Thus, though we cannot make our sun

Stand still, yet we make him run.

Chapter Thirty-Eight

"Grief is great. Only you and I in this land know that yet. Let us be good to one another."

A Year with Aslan, C. S. Lewis

After

Thursday 4/6

"A Memory Made of Light" was the title typed in darkest grey ink in the middle of the first white A4 sheet of paper: Nothing above or beneath it, nothing to suggest who had written it or what it was. Five words put together to initiate the suggestion of a story. Eighteen letters that in sequence would begin the unravelling of a tale that would by its finish, become the final, and in the end, most successful novel Arthur Valentine would ever write.

Held squarely in his large, gentle palms Ed spent a minute just assessing the weight of it. He could tell doing this, expert as he was, that it was almost three hundred pages long, one sided printed, one and a half spacing which was smaller than his contemporaries used but Arthur felt it reasonable as he often used plenty of return button tapping to create a lot of shorter paragraphs. He believed it read better, slower. And the older he got, the more responsible he wanted to be for the pace of his readers: An authoritative gesture, this fatherly function.

Carron had discussed the bare minimum of this work-so-far with Ed, focusing only on the author's dilemma expressed to her at the beginning of the week. Ed held this copy not knowing the plot or the characters, as yet unaware of the location or time frame it was pitched at. They would never take away from each other any fraction of that visceral, exciting initial read, especially from a new piece by their venerated Valentine.

Being that as it may, within Ed's hands was this original, fresh read. Something he relished above and beyond all other manuscript readings, and he settled himself upon his trusted old, soft couch. The warm glass of his favourite French Fleurie red wine had been poured into the glass on the table but sat there as yet un-sipped.

He cleared his brain of all else, everyday errands and other activities, time and space unchallenged, Ed took in a deep, calming breath and slowly pealed open the title sheet to reveal the beginning of Arthur's fifteenth (and final) work.

> 'It began as a beautiful Autumn Saturday. The date of our fortieth wedding Anniversary. We sat together in the glass conservatory as we had done almost every day for those treasured decades. We opened our cards to each other, smiling at our little in jokes, softening at loving words still written after so many years. And yet within that time, a singular moment passing from his arm reaching across the breakfast table picking up the milk jug, to the pouring of it into his cup of tea he had forgotten entirely who I was.
>
> We did not wake up that perfect morning expecting our world to be broken into a million pieces like the explosion of a planet, but that is, to us, was exactly what happened..."

And with those first few paragraphs Ed was hooked. The completion of this reading would take him just over four hours. It would be much shorter in normal circumstances but this was something special. Ed wanted to savour it, to experience the sighs and pangs of it. It was the honourable things to do to what he had already realised would be a new celebrated masterpiece.

Izzy watched through the reflection in the glass window, her eyes dipping with the temperate light as she studied Ed quietly. She felt concern. Looking at Ed through the window glaze reflection she could see he was twitchy with anticipation. His long leg had been tapping thoughtlessly whilst he settled himself eagerly down. She could see only one manuscript with him tonight: A singular piece. This was unusual indeed, Ed did not do change but yet these last few weeks he had displayed a worrying altering of their steady routine. She did not feel good about it. As unhappy as their new daily life had become at least there was some comfort in its stability.

But these new small changes, unexplained and distracted felt a further space between them. Izzy had enough about her to realise there was not a lot more that could happen so as to break them entirely. Their whole time had the frailty of those dainty eggshells just waiting to be shattered. A breath forever inhaled. A foot on a minefield bomb pending its weighted release.

"Why is it that one can never think of the past without wanting to go back?"

The Collected Letters of C. S. Lewis

So that you will hear me

my words

sometimes grow thin

as the tracks of the gulls on the beaches.

Necklace, drunken bell

for your hands smooth as grapes.

And I watch my words from a long way off.

They are more yours than mine.

They climb on my old suffering like ivy.

It climbs the same way on damp walls.

You are to blame for this cruel sport.

They are fleeting from my dark lair.

You fill everything, you fill everything.

Before you they peopled the solitude that you

   occupy,

and they are more used to my sadness than you are.

Now I want them to say what I want to say to you

to make you hear as I want you to hear me.

The wind of anguish still hauls on them as usual.

Sometimes hurricanes of dreams still knock them over.

You listen to other voices in my painful voice.

Lament of old mouths, blood of old supplications.

Love me, companion. Don't forsake me. Follow me.

Follow me, companion, on this wave of anguish.

But my words become stained with your love.

You occupy everything, you occupy everything.

I am making them into an endless necklace

for your white hands, smooth as grapes.

Chapter Thirty-Nine

"Her absence is like the sky, spread over everything. But no, that is not quite accurate. There is one place where her absence comes locally home to me, and it is a place I can't avoid. I mean my own body. It had such a different importance while it was the body of H.'s lover. Now it's like an empty house."

A Grief Observed, C. S. Lewis

After

Saturday 4/6

It was early Saturday morning. Izzy lay in bed awake with Ed still asleep, snoring softly beside her. His left arm folded behind his head whilst his right lay across his pale chest. She lay there staring at him in the half-dark. Watching his ribs rise and fall to his breathy sighs. She smelt the faint lemon soap on his warm skin from his shower hours before and it soothed her as nothing else did.

Four weeks had passed since Ed had been home late on Thursdays. It was hard for Izzy sometimes to tell which days were which in the week. She was just always tired, all the time; so exhausted: How tiring it was in her muddled brain to remember, or how arduous forgetting. The hours were long and the house was identical, evenings after his work kept their same routines of door open, bag down, kiss on head, dinner prepared and eaten then Ed reading from his pile of papers until eleven when he packed up ready for bed and she would faithfully, silently, follow.

Four whole weeks, was a lengthy expanse when nothing distinguishable occurred in reality. Those unexplained extra two hours Thursday delay created more of an impact than either of them expected. Izzy was unnerved. Ed was as attentive as ever but something invisible had shifted between them, a new state of play.

On the first three occasions Ed was his ever gentle self as he sat beside her and watched her tenderly as she slowly nibbled at his carefully grilled cheese toasts, lovingly prepared with beautiful ingredients. It was a shame then that to Izzy it all tasted of paste and dust. No flavours or joy could she muster with her mouth-full lacklustre sense. Everything was simply variety of textures to chew and swallow, painstakingly sluggishly. She had long ago lost her hunger, lost that feeling of being sated, of delicious replete. She took no pleasure in this absence of these daily enjoyments. It stuck firm in her mind that she didn't have the strength to pretend even for Ed's benefit, that his hard work was worthwhile. All those times when they sat eating together, so physically near yet it was as if they had miles stretched between them. And as she lay there all those nights in bed, only inches away, it might well have been an entire country apart, so impossible it would feel to reach over and connect. These were only some of her failings as a wife she could add to the long list stored so ashamedly inside.

She refused the pills the doctors had prescribed in case she would miss out on their child's virtual visits; in case taking them erased the only thread of imagination that made her days mean anything. The clarity of her controlled day-dreamed world was vivid and believable, if only for herself, beginning from the closing on the front door out until the opening of it again. It was Izzy's consolation and her diversion. It was her choice and her protection against what was before and what might be now if she was ever brave enough to ask.

But..but..these late Thursdays. These changes, his deviation was worrying. That trace in the air, that wisp of shame that flashed across his eyes when he thought she didn't notice in the glass reflection. The harder he kissed her hair on those evenings, unknown to him, just by a fraction but to Izzy it was as raw as a burn. When silence is all you have. When other senses have gone away you notice everything else. Nothing is by accident or without intent. In a sharper sensory world of heighten vision and touch Izzy observed every single part of Ed and this variation was disturbing. So long had she spent away from him in spirit and in noise that she had now felt her confidence misplaced assuming his continued strength and support and this shook her deeply. It very much frightened her.

Two nights ago was the fourth Thursday he was anonymously delayed and Ed was definitely bothered by something. Something lay behind his generous, grey eyes that was like a question she couldn't answer, the floating spoke of a dandelion clock she couldn't quite catch. His kiss had been a lighter touch, his patience with her soup eating limited and perfunctory, not to say unkind but certainly distracted, aloof. And when he studied the first and only manuscript he had brought home that night, he repeatedly broke off from his fervent reading and looked away, towards the wall, focussing on nothing in particular but simply staring into the space as if waiting for something that never appeared.

She never realised how heavy sorrow weighed by having it wrapped around her skin like armour. The marble shell of her that had for almost a year trapped her safely inside, now began to feel suffocating and menacing, not protective and stable. Its grip was tightening, closing in. She wanted to tell Ed, to explain. She wanted to scream, she wanted to break it off all around her like hard boots slamming into an iced puddle splintering the top. She wanted to wriggle out of it like a chrysalis gasping for free air. She wanted to not be so tired, so goddamn weak. She desperately wanted him to touch her. To feel his strong arms around her and split through the invisible, tough casing that held her firm but ever-separate from him.

Izzy watched him now, still sleeping, so close. Her eyes looked at his familiar profile, the small fresh blond hairs dotted around his morning jawline, the straight, seamless line of his nose, the curves of his lips, which pulled at her hurt heart, his sweet, caring lips not kissed enough.

The muscles around her lungs begin to constrict and it seemed to take a herculean effort to raise her right hand, just the tiniest amount, towards him: Unaware as he was. And she suddenly knew that the sadness she overwhelmingly felt at that precise moment was not the three kisses that were firmer on her head in his welcome home but rather the fragility of that fourth.

This momentous awareness from the small, impalpable fragments she herself had translated gave her a fierce sense of trying, a cracking of the shield. She loved him. She did love him so. Her hand moved with further strength and touched his own; lightly at first so as not to startle him but becoming ever pressing as the seconds wore on.

Ed breathed in a deep long sigh and instinctively turned his head towards her, his eyes blinking open in the semi-light to look over, to check as always, if she was alright. It took him only a moment longer to realise they were holding hands. His big, strong palm had automatically grabbed hers within it, a gesture as natural to him as blinking.

In the haze of those daybreak hours Ed was confused, it felt surreal and dream-like to be lying touching her again from her suggestion, after so long, after so much. Izzy felt exposed and alert. She had started this act but now was unsure of how to continue. Ed looked deeper into her, sensing her nervousness yet noticing also a spark of resolve somewhere in the colour of her big, hopeful eyes. The sensation of her soft hand in his felt glorious and he stroked it slowly with the tip of his thumb as if it was the first time he'd ever held her: Delicate, soundless.

Izzy moved her head towards his, closer, so close that their mouths touched and their lips parted in faultless synchronicity as only old lovers know. He kissed her softly and gently, taking his time, every subtle urge waiting for its consented response. Soon their tongues were inside each other, searching and determined, remembering the motions of how they first found each other. Arousing a reddening heat across Izzy's cheeks, her neck and down through her now supple body into her excited breasts, the forgotten dampening between her legs.

Ed carefully released her hand so as to put his own up to her face, under her ears, holding her cheeks safely and treasured, savouring every lap and curl. It was a few moments before Izzy leaned in further still, changing her kisses into nuzzles over his jaw and high up by his neck. Aware she could not hear anything, no noise at all as Izzy whispered in a hoarse, quivering voice, feeble with lack of use, and asked,

"May……. I……. Touch…….?"

And Ed fell open into her loving butterflied body, free and adoring, hoping she would be able only to notice his willing, tender actions towards her from devoted husband to inviting wife - not his grateful, fallen tear he tried hard to hold back but couldn't keep in.

It had taken so much out of her that first time that for a few minutes after their love making Izzy had rested herself upon him with an empty mind. Her usually crammed and over-flowing dark thoughts cleared momentarily leaving her a few calm moments of peace.

She thought only of her shuddering muscles pulsing within her, slowing down into a low hum of carnal satisfaction, its blissful reward. A slick of sweat between them, from each or one of them shared, it was impossible to know so entangled they were now.

Ed's large strong arms pulled her in close like he ever did, her silken hair tucking under his chin filling him with the scent of her again, cherished and wanted. His own body spent and throbbing gently with the thrill of their sensual movements. Quiet together and yet together at last. For once the shared silence did not seem to burn into them with its guilty intensity.

This brief respite was unexpected for Izzy as she turned her head and placed it gently on the left side of his chest momentarily. And it was then she remembered. As violent and as fierce as a punch to her neck, as if cracking her windpipe and startling her with no breath or air. She heard it as she always did. With no aids, no aural assistance, the sound still came through right into her and shocked her like charged electric heart paddles: A bolt of lightning energy, hot and white; that pounding noise, their created throbbing sound, that alarming-alive reminder that could never be untied.

Izzy stayed where she lay, against him, listening to that familiar muted rhythm, that perfect sound-full beat and she couldn't help herself but weep. Her tears fell first in small drips and then flowed further out and on Ed's naked body but she did not move away. He heard her muffled sobbing and felt the rocking of her shoulders as she cried. He kissed her long hair and moved his arms in towards her, enclosing her safe within them like protecting a lost, frail star. He did not move away.

The glass bird swung unseen above them. It moved to the exact pulse of the husband's heartbeat. It swayed to the identical tempo of the wife's tears. Only it knew that they were both going at precisely the same pace.

"Grief is like a long valley, a winding valley where any bend may reveal a totally new landscape."

C. S. Lewis, A Grief Observed

FACT:

The hearts of a couple in love start to synchronise after the

couple have looked into each other's eyes for three minutes.

Chapter Forty

"The primary function of poetry, as of all the arts, is to make us more aware of ourselves and the world around us. I do not know if such increased awareness makes us more moral or more efficient. I hope not. I think it makes us more human, and I am quite certain it makes us difficult to deceive."

W. H. Auden

After

Kidlington Presbytery,

Oxfordshire

Dear Eddie,

Thank you for your generous email to our group. It was very touching to read how you are still trying to find ways of helping Isobel. I'm sorry that the Doctors and Therapists don't seem to have worked after almost a year. Grief can be a cruel and frightening business. No two people deal with it the same.

I know you have been at home looking after Isobel alongside working at the office. Your abundance of love is wonderful to behold. Your faith in your vows of marriage, your faith in your wife is as compassionate as it is honourable. I hope you feel the strength and support from us all and more also from your other city friends and colleagues.

I am booked to visit Isobel next week and sit with her for a few hours, as before. I'm glad to be of some use whilst she is on her own in the week day times. At the moment I can manage travelling up bi-monthly for this. I wish I could do more.

There are some passages from various theological books and essays I read in the silence to Isobel but if you like I am open to take advice from you as to what else to recite.

She does not respond of course, but I do feel she is aware of my company and presence. Some of my parishioners and those in the community I work with require company and quiet companionship rather than conversation. I am happy to do either.

On our last phone call you mentioned her Uncle had sent some books from her childhood over and I thought maybe picking one of these might be suitable. Sometimes it is in our children's stories that so much in adult life is explained to us.

Our Oxford college loyalties give us a wealth of authors to choose from, leaning us to the Tolkeins and the Lewis' compilations, for good reason of course but perhaps I could begin with Carroll's Alice. A girl lost in another world with the hope of coming back home again. It could be an adventure she would enjoy and even, dare we hope, inspire. One of Carroll's own quotes is written on a postcard I keep on my mantel which says; "One of the secrets of life is that all that is really worth the doing is what we do for others." and I keep it there because it reminds my visitors, of all ages, all cultures and religions, that there is a cord of kindness that that exists between us all, no matter our backgrounds or beliefs and I hope it is this which I can offer to the many. What a fine achievement that would be.

But let me return again to your initial ask; to your thoughtful mission. Aren't we so lucky to have the joy of Poetry to unite and ignite us. More and more I go back to the shelves of our Poets to shine a light on this world, on its modernity, on humanity. The trouble is from too much wonderment where to decide upon. Our Aslan journeys have taken us over and across the landscape of poetry and poets and yet still there is so much more we have yet to discover: This is the joy, the colossal undertaking, the very privilege available to us, our poetry-kin.

My choice is included below. I offer one to yourself, the inimitable Robert Frost, whose classic piece never fails to leave a weight on my chest upon reading. Not a threatening pressure but more of a firm hold of hand above heart. I feel this is a gesture of solidarity from one person to another, as he recounts the idea of somebody else going through an event similar to another, that human bond.

For Isobel I enclose a Mary Oliver one. It was a joy to me finding such a remarkable woman poet whose lines resonate and haunt me as much as any rousing sermon.

Eddie, I see how gentle you are with her. I witness how kind and tender you behave, even though you must also be struggling with the burden of grieving. I very much admire how you have conducted yourself throughout this. You have shown remarkable strength and decency.

I hope you feel we are all behind you and beside you as you carry on. I wish to send you all my love, thoughts and prayers. You are never alone.

Talk soon,

Geoffrey

"If a poet has to save his soul, he may save the soul of others."

Richard Eberhart

The Journey – Mary Oliver

One day you finally knew

what you had to do, and began,

though the voices around you

kept shouting

their bad advice –

though the whole house

began to tremble

and you felt the old tug

at your ankles.

"Mend my life!"

each voice cried.

But you didn't stop.

You knew what you had to do,

though the wind pried

with its stiff fingers

at the very foundations,

though their melancholy

was terrible.

It was already late

enough, and a wild night,

and the road full of fallen

branches and stones.

But little by little,

as you left their voices behind,

the stars began to burn

through the sheets of clouds,

and there was a new voice

which you slowly

recognised as your own,

that kept you company

as you strode deeper and deeper

into the world,

determined to do

the only thing you could do –

determined to save

the only thing you could save.

Acquainted With The Night - Robert Frost

I have been acquainted with the night.

I have walked out in the rain – and back in rain.

I have outwalked the furthest city light.

I have looked down the saddest city lane.

I have passed the watchman on his beat

And dropped my eyes, unwilling to explain.

I have stood still and stopped the sound of feet

When far away an interrupted cry

Came over houses from another street,

But not to call me back or say goodbye;

And further still as an unearthly height,

A luminary clock against the sky.

Proclaimed the time was neither wrong or right,

I have been acquainted with the night.

Chapter Forty-One

"Night, the beloved. Night when words fade and things come alive. When the destructive analysis of day is done, and all that is truly important becomes whole at sound again. When man reassembles his fragmentary self and grows with the calm of a tree."

Antoine de Saint-Exupery

After

Since that morning panic when Izzy had initiated sex with Ed it had become a nightly habit. No personal words or language out loud occurred still. They were just getting used to their bodies again, touch, stroke, embrace.

The daytimes were still filled with her other world existence but something seismic had shifted and it was impossible to feel settled to her stomach the way she once had been. Tearing the two sections of daily life cleanly in half, separate and distinct; one a mother, one a wife, however unsuccessful she felt in being both, didn't seem to be possible anymore. It was starting to feel like the beginning of the end for one of those roles of her, but for now she was unable to know which one.

Since Izzy's exterior shell had been cracked wide open she was becoming overwhelming in her desire for Ed. It was as if all those endless months had been gathered in and sped up to a desperation of intimacy. Every second over that year and more that she wanted but couldn't break free to hold him close or kiss him back, she now remembered as vivid as a cold twisting grip upon her arms pushing her down, and the only relief she had to stop that guilt and angst was to now begin again: To truly look towards his face, direct and honest, without the filter of that front room window reflection: To *see* him and for him to feel seen.

As much as this loving physicality between them was their new normal it still had its constraints. There were unsaid rules they had to respect and honour. So frightened were they to change or challenge these for fear something of this new unspoken magic could disappear as quickly as it began, they continued the timeframe of waiting until their traditional, silent and separate evenings were ending before they closed down the day and headed for their bedroom together.

Hands now held as they once ever did when they walked together *before*, leaving that aloof, stationary front room that embodied their distance and division. The short walk to their bedroom began with a gentle caressing of each other's fingers and wrists in anticipation. Neither of them knew on each of these fresh nights, who first reached out to start their touching. It was impossible to remember or distinguish so woven were they now, stitched together in their dissolving of the once cold space between them.

When they were dating, all those years ago, Izzy would write Ed stories, short little pages, handwritten and thoughtful. They began simply as little love notes, a paragraph maybe about something beautiful she had discovered about him and what that meant to her. Quite soon after these became longer and more insightful. They occurred so many times over the course of their early years as there seemed to Izzy so much to say, so many things to be grateful for: a thousand tiny actions and behaviours that she wished to give thanks to.

You bought my favourite coffee. It was the same brand my Mother used to drink, in one of the few memories I have of her. I mentioned it briefly, only once when we were talking about so many other things that long morning walk by the river, but you had kept hold of this small part and quietly remembered it. So weeks later, when we ran drenched and laughing back to your house after being caught in that surprising Autumn storm, you made me a cup, without glory or show, you made me that cup of coffee to warm me up and make me smile.

They say that memories are woken with familiar senses and that divine gesture flooded me not with tears of loss but with a wave of tender care and heartfelt safety. The way you remember, that part of you that thinks of such perfect things, humble and profound, makes it so easy to love you; makes your love so very valuable. It makes being loved by you my very favourite part of living in this enormous and beckoning world. And I smile. I smile for you and because of you.

I.

Thank.

You. X

Ed would find them in various places around the house, in the closed bureau dresser when he went to find a pen, in a coat jacket pocket when he was searching for his keys, on his bedside table as he settled down for the night, those few nights they were apart, wishing she was lying beside him.

I adored the way you kissed my hair this morning on your way to work when you thought I was sleeping. I wish we could repeat last night and all its perfect moments. Today will seem warmer as I sit on the train home thinking about our yesterday adventures. And it will feel colder the further the train moves away, like those clues for children's hide and seek games. You are sun and fire and joy and stars. I will miss you tonight. I will miss your kisses that will not wake me up tomorrow morning.

You are so very good at kisses.

See.

You.

Soon. X

On their first wedding anniversary she went to Maxwell Bookbinders and had them bound up into a hand-held tan leather volume. Now Izzy closed her eyes and recalled his reaction when he opened it over dinner that Friday evening. His kind, loving eyes widened with curiosity as his fingers brushed the soft cover gently and in those five seconds between him pulling back the cover and realising what private treasures she had kept safe close inside for him to keep forever seemed eternal. The change from his wonder to his initial reading then to the understanding at the breadth of her thoughtfulness and care printed and sewn tight in that gift was an incredible moment Izzy would play and re-play exactly, repeating the same elation of that time, as clear and as sensuous to her as reading an old, favourite phrase.

Today Izzy was restless and agitated. After their first week of intimacy, Izzy tried to think on it, decipher the difference of why something so important had changed and what that now meant. She was too feeble to get up and find a pen and paper to write down her impressions on. This visual communication that their marriage enjoyed has ceased, like so much, since *before.* Izzy thought of what she would write. In her head she watched herself form the words onto a piece of make-believe paper and inscribe her new thoughts into a letter for Ed. Thoughts she needed to put down to try and make sense of them for herself too. A letter that clarified her beliefs and fears behind the silent wall she hid behind, alone. A letter Ed would never be able to read.

I want to be near you, in bedtime, in the darkness, when the sanity of the daylight hours have disappeared. It feels possible only then to join with you, without being scrutinised under the strong glare of the jealous sun. Daylight is too intense, too demanding, as if we're auditioning for roles in a perfect family play, the choreography of expected daily life. It's under the careless moon that we are freed. The matte, navy shadows envelop us, un-judgemental; our expressions unclear under the low beam, like restless spies looking for clues from a stranger.

I find you here, where silence is approved of. Your joyous, working, muscular body remains steady and calm and I feel all the possible harsh verdicts and burning, anguished questions seep away willingly as my hungry mouth devours the salty taste of you. We release ourselves from all those diurnal tortured hours our brains create and simply stop; indulging in the consolation our functioning bodies compose together, hot and sticky, wet and hard.

My orgasm moaning is the only noise I make to you and you have stopped trying to quieten this with your fevered kisses. You relish in it, you wish for it, welcoming the very guttural sounds you have made me achieve either by your firm, masculine shape, your feather-like tongue or deft and expert fingers. And when we are both left gasping and spent, those beautiful seconds of twinning with another human being, I let you gather me in for my most beloved part.

I never explain to you why I crave you close. I want to say it is because I have to be near you. To reach in and touch you as both comfort and solace in our joint hours of need. I want to tell you that it is my infinite love for you that makes me rest into your steady heartbeat; the very proof you are still here even though she is not.

And I love you, I do, I do, I do. And yet…what I am scared to say is, that I knew, from the very first magical scan, until our very last time of hearing through the midwife's machine, I could hear her own heart beat and it was yours. Not mine or a new sound but one equivalent and identical to your own. In listening to you I can imagine I'm listening to her, your child, made from our bodies, following your very same rhythmic drum.

And we lie together in absolute hush except that brilliance of your sound, our damp and exhausted bodies together you loving me and I loving her still. Will it always be this way? I yearn to ask it, but my throat makes no sound, it's frozen. I realise it must be because I do not want you to answer that question. Please, please don't.

And all my broken, futile, voice-less mouth is now good for is when I connect it to your own with our silent kisses; through them I hope to project the stories I wish I could tell you, my lonely tales for us. I wish you can understand and translate them, those many chapters we could still be. I want you to know their endings. Yet even if you do not hear them in my silence, I hope you still will always kiss me back.

Your kisses. You are so good at kisses.

I.

Miss.

You.   X

"There is a place in the heart that

will never be filled

and

we will wait

and

wait

there in that space."

Charles Bukowski

If You Forget Me

"I want you to know

one thing.

You know how this is:

if I look

at the crystal moon, at the red branch

of the slow autumn at my window,

if I touch

hear the fire

the impalpable ash

or the wrinkled body of the log,

everything carries me to you,

as if everything that exists,

aromas, lights, metals,

were little boats

that sail

towards those isles that wait for me.

Well, now,

if little by little you stop loving me

I shall stop loving you little by little.

If suddenly

you forget me

do not look for me,

for I shall already have forgotten you.

If you think it long and mad,

The wind of banners

That passes through my life,

and you decide

to leave me at the shore

of the heart where I have roots,

remember

that on that day,

at that hour,

I shall lift my arms

and my roots will set off

to seek another land…"   Pablo Neruda

Chapter Forty-Two

"Lay your sleeping head, my love,

Human on my faithless arm;

Time and fevers burn away

Individual beauty from

Proves the child ephemeral:

But in my arms till break of day

Let the living creatures lie,

Mortal, guilty, but to me

The entirely beautiful.

Soul and body have no bounds:

To lovers as they lie upon

Her tolerant enchanted slope

In their ordinary swoon,

Grave the vision Venus sends

Of supernatural sympathy,

Universal love and hope;

While abstract insight wakes

Among the glaciers and the rocks

The hermit's sensual ecstacy…"

Lullaby, W.H. Auden (part one)

After

Monday after 4/6

It was just before closing time on the Monday back at work and Ed knocked on Carron's open office door. She was sat behind her large desk, her glasses beside the multiple sheets on her desk, her fingers lifted from typing on the keyboard in front of her.

Beckoning him in with a wide smile Carron gestured for Ed to take a seat in the armchairs so familiar to them now. She was not surprised to see the document he placed on the table there as he slowly sat himself down.

Ed's right hand rubbed against his forehead as if pressing that area could somehow penetrate right through the skull bones, causing his brain to jolt itself into an answer. Arthur Valentine was an author of high standing and to be invited as his editors, to make a decision about his work, especially one so imperative to the story, felt a heavy-weighted responsibility. Carron lifted the glass bottle of Whiskey but Ed shook his head in refusal.

"Thank you but not tonight. I've been reading and re-reading the story all week and am struggling to keep my head clear as to what can be done. It's so simply and perfectly written and yet the answer to his storyline seems far away to me."

"Yes, he has composed a truly beautiful dilemma. There is no right or wrong way as people will be hurt whichever the choice. Arthur has such a gift about life and chance."

Despite all the many possible opportunities available that the main characters could defer, somehow to Ed there seemed ultimately only two. Robert Frost had been right all along. Should Erika, the wife stay with the husband she loved with the very real likelihood he would never recover and know her, their life as a couple forever damaged? Or would she leave him for the kindly Doctor who had a fair future ahead and a willing and open heart to offer her, the potential of new love again?

"The characters are real and flawed. The way he has shown us how they all made it to the present situation without clues to what could happen in their futures is such a challenge to both the heart and the brain." Ed considered.

Upon now knowing these well-explained people and their own personable histories, there felt no third or more options. Both roads were absolute. Once a decision had been made and that line crossed over there would be no chance of going back. Something intrinsic would be lost, a thread broken. The obligation to these people, however fictitious, felt immense and profound, and timewise this decision faced felt palpable and urgent.

The book was not written as a moral tale it was simply a story about a man, his wife and a possible new love. It was as honest as life itself. Valentine wrote with no judgement or punishment for the parties involved. It was just an account, a simple chronicle of what could be happening anywhere across the world to anybody in it. He was so talented at siphoning out the frailties in precious situations and the impact of deliberations from uncontrolled events.

The unfinished manuscript sat on the table between Ed and Carron, almost throbbed for attention, like a new bruise, dark and beckoning. Carron stood up from the armchair opposite and walked up and down the back wall. She wanted to stretch her legs and back after so many long hours stooped over her desk or tucked back into those office chairs on various phone calls and business chats. Like Ed, her mind was swollen to the point of un-clarity. The future prospects available for the book cast, from such tangled relationships and internal beliefs all woven together were overwhelming.

Not for the first time Carron was grateful it was not her job to be an Author. To be in charge of other's lives, to play God even to those who weren't real, unlocked a cacophony of problems and dramas that were continuous in their ever-changing plights.

Carron was a successful single woman, no children, siblings or pets, even her elderly parents were in considered good health so outside of work, of which there were more than a few needy clients, there were no dependants she ever had to be relied on or about. She was extremely good at her job, an enormous asset to Fallon House, with her firm but fair handling of vital and sensitive clients and colleagues. But perhaps with someone who has not been personally touched with any of the worlds more unpredictable or imbalanced circumstances, it is hard to understand that things are more complicated than what is written down succinctly in the pages of a hardback. Rarely were lives so clear and fair.

Her tolerance of people she considered emotionally weaker, was minimal. This was a huge asset in her business world, setting up a remarkable work ethic and standard of production. It also, despite all the books she had ever read, all the stories of lives she had not herself lived, made her perhaps emotionally naive in the realities of actual life. As much as she understood and enjoyed the many Author's work of plot charting, deliberate angsts and fraught situations most of these ended with a satisfying result, a sense of justice or closure. It feels some writer's job to present a tangled pile of sticks, like the childhood game, and commit their following lines to carefully picking each part off the other until the underneath is revealed and the wooden poles lined up neatly together. The reader exhales a sigh of satisfaction, puzzle completed, lesson by osmosis, learned.

But also Carron would of course come across another type of writer who would present a snapshot of lives and decipher emotions or reasons within that were compassionate or explainable but the outcome of events remained upsettingly unchallenged. The story of a situation that the characters were powerless to change but swept along a fated route as the reader watched, themselves helpless, to affect a different outcome. These would leave Carron unsettled. They would ask more questions than they answered, illicit unkind emotions without intention to soothe or repair. These were the books when she would gasp not sigh at that final closed page. They were not always her favourite but she still knew they had significant value in their telling. Most often she learned more after reading this type of novel than the ones with happier endings.

"Arthur Valentine has requested we have no longer than these two weeks on settling this quandary. This will give him the time he needs for re-writing and getting it approved and sent off to the printers ready for the important spring promotion next year."

"If we both use these up-coming Thursdays after work hours, if that of course is alright with you Carron, to spend some hours going through it that could bring us up to the deadline for a decision. This should be plenty of time to come to a conclusion for him." Ed surmised.

"Ideal. That's great, I'll make some notes for this week." Carron said as she retrieved her own copy of the manuscript, taking the fresh, lined pad off her desk and placed the two together on her lap.

In reality this asking could not have come at a worse time in all the years Carron and Ed had known and worked together. The professional area of merging private and personal empathies and theories in open discussions felt in one way, highly inappropriate yet in another, incredibly relevant.

Perhaps it was the forced circumstance, given further time the two of them could have tackled these emotive subjects gently and sensitively over the months and longer. Small droplets of words, fragments of questions and subtle answers over party drinks or coffee runs: Maybe even those relaxed ten minutes once meetings had concluded which led to general chit chat disclosing information of the everyday; a casual intimacy, that softer link.

"I'll do the same and we can review it then. Thanks so much Carron." Ed started to get up from the chair.

"Are you sure you won't stay a little?" she offered. The scent of the recently oiled walnut table was musty and old. The lined wall of Fallon's published books, all editions and translations looked safe and relaxing. Nothing here was confusing or complicated. In this space he felt that he knew about this fixed and steady world and his judgement could be actioned and trusted. He was confident under this city roof, truthful within these brick walls.

"Maybe next time" Ed answered with a sigh. It was all too easy to stay but was it right? He wondered.

Ed left to go home. He would be back on time, no delay or concern. Carron remained in her chair, the manuscript and pad within arm's reach, her mind whirling with dark thoughts of story endings.

There was no invisible bird above to watch them here. There was no witness to these times. There were no glass eyes or ears to see and hear what was happening in the in-between hours when Ed wasn't at home, about that in-between book plot line from that Author that knew them so well, or to notice those words unsaid in-between the others they had spoken out loud.

"What is that you express in your eyes? It seems to me more than all the print I have read in my life."

Walt Whitman

Chapter Forty-Three

"Death opens a door out of a little, dark room (that's all the life we have known before it) into a great, real place where the true sun shines and we shall meet."

Till We Have Faces, C. S. Lewis

After

Thursday 5/6 am

It was a Thursday again. She had come to recognise it in various ways. How Ed's face was more drawn in the mornings as he gathered the previous evening's manuscripts back into his leather satchel. How he distractedly cleared away his breakfast plate, leaving small fragments of toast crumbs dotted around the kitchen surface, never left behind on other days.

His goodbye kiss was softer and the manner in which he shut the front door on his way to work, invisible to her eye, clicked tighter somehow into the lock leaving behind a sense in the room as if it might not ever get back opened.

But mostly, for Izzy, it was the urgency of his touches those nights before. He seemed less satisfied, more wanting as they lay together silently. She could taste the desperation in the warm air from him as he searched deeper into her anxious green eyes, kissed further into her mouth as if he could lick up stolen words within it and they would appear on his own tongue like desired answers.

His dreams were light and fitful and he woke as if he had not slept at all. And when she lay her heart upon his chest on those Wednesdays in the dark, it beat faster than its natural pace, which in turn made hers race. It was a sound she did not like. It was a noise that did not represent what it always did.

That morning Izzy went to the bookshelf in the front room and looked through until she found the one she most wanted to read. It was an old poem she remembered from when her father had told it to her, so very long ago now. A poem so incredibly matched to her own self now and then, before and before, that it felt like a secret note written just to her. So private that message, so lonely her grief, yet some timeworn verses seemed as true to her today as if she had imagined them from that poet to her own self.

Her thin, gentle fingers brushed through the brown edged paper pages until she reached the list of first lines. Izzy believed she could recall the correct one from this initial start. Her heart leapt the moment she found it, her breath caught and before she lost her nerve she brought the book with her to the day chair by the window, it was caught in the morning sun-stream.

She lay with her legs outstretched and her arms cradling the book carefully as if it was a precious spell. Was she able to read it out loud? She didn't think so. Perhaps a little, maybe she should practise? Iz hesitated and decided to wait and read it to herself first, just her, sat there all alone.

A Poem for Emily – W. H. Auden

Small fact and fingers and farthest one from me,

a hand's width and two generations away,

in this still present I am fifty-three.

You are not yet a full day.

When I am sixty-three, when you are ten,

and you are neither closer nor as far,

your arms will fill with what you know by then,

the arithmetic and love we do and are.

When I by blood and luck am eighty-six

And you are some place thirty-three

believing in sex and god and politics

with children who look not at all like me,

some time I know you will have read them this

so they will know I love them and say so

and love their mother. Child, whatever is

is always or never was. Long ago,

a day I watched a while beside your bed,

I wrote this down, a thing that might be kept

a while, to tell you what I would have said

when you were know knows what and I was dead

which is I stood and loved you while you slept.

Izzy placed the book down carefully and closed her eyes, letting them bathe in the warm
sun as the pretty curtains moved with the light breeze. She thought of each line carefully,
with study and awe and felt the after-glow of its perfection touch her like the closing hum

of a prayer. Its words whispering all around her, that original Auden voice owning each verse with his hoarse, throated character; haunting her with his truth and confessions as if he had taken her very life and described it back to her. Izzy thought and doze, considered and napped.

She hardly felt the cheeks of the toddler lean upon her legs as its little face looked up towards her Mum, hearing in that air every un-said word of the poem. Realising what it might mean before Izzy did: Those small, chubby arms squeezing against Izzy's knees to look for comfort or notice but to no avail. That tiny ghost-girl standing and loving her while she slept.

Oh that poor bird looked down upon them. Oh how it wished that it could fly. It swung to pull on itself, to check again the strength of its wire but with no feathered wings, no working mouth what was the point? The helplessness felt painful. Bearing witness to such grief with its curved pathways and twisted corners was awful to watch. Such sadness that it did not know the outcome, the last written page of this story, how could it impact their plot?

It closed its eyes and slowly rocked as it listened to the soft, soul-aching sobbing, gentle and quiet, in that room they all shared, and it genuinely did not know if it came from the woman, the young ghost-girl or its own self.

"For the greater the love the greater the grief."

C. S. Lewis, A Grief Observed

Chapter Forty-Four

"A poet's work is to name the unnameable, to point at frauds, to take sides, start arguments,

shape the world, and stop it going to sleep."

Salman Rushdie

After

ASLAN EMAIL   Re: Help

Dear Edward,

My apologies for the late reply, I have been on a Writers Retreat in the northern part of America for almost a month. No phones, no internet, no contact. So as I sit here now returned to my office going through the backlogs of emails, letters and messages, and I discovered your touching request. Please forgive my tardiness.

I am sorry to hear that Isobel is still in such a dark place about the world. Death of a loved one, even one not met yet, cannot fail to have an intensely deep effect.

I am very proud at your belief in the power of words at such a time. I know they have been a huge source of comfort and relief for myself and of course many others over the years.

Having lived over the Atlantic now for as long as I have, I should perhaps offer a suggestion from one of their own eminent and very worthy poets. Whitman, of course, springs to mind immediately, as does the beloved Frost. I imagine you must have already been offered some from the great cummings. (I would bet he was Andrew's prime candidate of choice).

If I may suggest perhaps a work of Maya Angelou, as my poem to you both; I feel she is haunting with her emotional honesty and I find her writings on issues of the heart both insightful and fearless.

I had the great privilege of seeing her once. By chance she was doing a book signing in Massachusetts, near the campus. Her book 'Phenomenal Women' had not long been published and I had purchased a copy. That old adage of not meeting your heroes certainly couldn't have been further from the truth. I found her warm, intelligent and delightful company. We spent almost an hour together discussing the relevance of Poetry in modern day society. I remember everything she spoke about and have directly quoted her in my lectures a great deal ever since.

One thing we both very much agreed on was the absolute importance of Poems, the transcendence of intentions and emotions it can achieve above all others; certainly at vital cruxes in life when other options seem unable to reach inside the absolute core of us, and help us in the very way we need most. She would indeed be a remarkable Aslan member.

Speaking of which, I enclose a poem by the great Czech poet Jaroslav Seifert for you as I am very much moved on his thoughts about his own work. I hope you take some inspiration or solace from his piece too.

I've never seen more beautiful Autumns than in this State, strikingly beautiful, a cornucopia of colours. Even the Springtime seems brighter and more perfumed than home. Were he ever here, Keats would no doubt have been inspired to re-write.

Feel free to come and visit if you think it would be helpful. I'd be delighted to host you both and show you the world of American Academia. You might even get tempted to stay. Publishing over here is extensive and exciting. You my boy, would be in your element.

Please do come back to me if you need anything else. My thoughts are to you two at this ongoing difficult time.

Your friend,

Henry

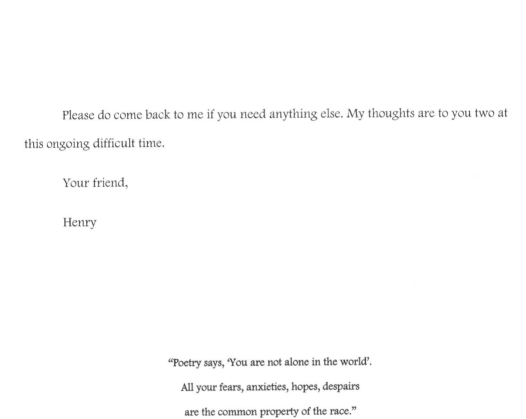

"Poetry says, 'You are not alone in the world'.
All your fears, anxieties, hopes, despairs
are the common property of the race."
Stanley Kunitz

Touched By An Angel — Maya Angelou

We, unaccustomed to courage

exiles from delight

live coiled in shells of loneliness

until love leaves its high holy temple

and comes into our sight

to liberate us into life.

Love arrives

and in its train comes ecstasies

old memories of pleasure

ancient histories of pain.

Yet if we are bold,

love strikes away the strains of fear

from our souls.

We are weaned from our timidity

in the flush of love's light

we dare be brave

and suddenly we see

That love costs all we are

And will ever be.

Yet it is only love

That sets us free.

To all those million verses in the world

I've added just a few.

They probably were no wiser than a cricket's chirrup.

I know. Forgive me.

I'm coming to the end.

They weren't even the first footmarks

in the lunar dust.

If at times they sparkled after all

it was not their light.

I love this language.

And that which forces silent lips

to quiver

will make young lovers kiss

as they stroll through red-gilded fields

under a sunset

slower than the tropics.

Poetry is with us from the start.

Like loving,

like hunger, like the plague, like war.

At times my verses were embarrassingly foolish.

But I make no excuse.

I believe that seeking beautiful words

is better

than killing and murdering.

"the great advantage of being alive

(instead of undying) is not so much

that mind no more can disprove than prove

what heart may feel and soul may touch

- the great (my darling) happens to be

that love are in we, that love are in we…"

ee cummings

Before

The edition of ee cummings 'selected poems 1923-58' had been one of Izzy's birthday gifts to Ed. By this time they had already been together eight months. She had sourced a magnificent first edition from the initial print run in 1969. Izzy had asked Alex to help with his American contacts in Boston to see if they could trace the best quality book they could find their end and post it over as most of the British copies she found weren't in the best condition and she wanted this to be as unspoiled as possible.

It arrived with two days to spare. It was delightfully packaged, wrapped with amongst other things, pages of a local newspaper reporting on their recent music festival, a photograph postcard of the Smithsonian written on the back by the bookseller, his own favourite cummings line, "there's a hell of a good universe next door…" and a small book of American stamps with pictures of Nasa's achievements upon them. Izzy couldn't help but smile at these, associating the space images with the postcard's travel themed famous quote.

The paperback itself looked perfect. Its cover had the name and year block printed on the front overlapping its colours. The texture of the covering cardboard was glossy and smooth to touch; it had hardly any chaffing or rounding at the corner's ninety degree cut angle; sharp and precise as if it had been placed tightly on a safe shelf without ever been looked at again.

A small ink portrait of the poet which sat in the first fold of the opening page depicted a soft, considerate face, cumming's large full lips closed towards their greying edges and his eyes seemed wise and knowing.

Izzy's heart did a slight dance at the joy of it all. This really was an electricity of excitement only felt by true lovers of all things Book. She knew immediately that Ed would be thrilled and she placed it carefully back inside the brown paper parcel, quite literally tied up with string, as she could think of no better way to present it to him than how it had arrived to her that day.

The importance to them both of cumming's 'may I touch' poem many months before, which began the secrets of their three word codes was a definitive moment. So it was that cummings became the poet that represented to them not just a great linking of their intellectual passions but very much of the sensual ones too.

Years before when Ed was asked at a dinner party to name his top three Poets he had laughed off the impossibility of narrowing them down but only because he did not want to reveal to someone else something he felt was absolutely private. He believed it to be such an intimate confession and yet when Isobel had suggested this very same question only one week from meeting each other and his reply to her was immediate.

Ed had simplified it so. "Neruda for Heart Love, cummings for Physical Love and Auden for Human Love." She had giggled with such preciseness. She was happy at his generosity to share this significant information and her flashing emerald eyes shone true warmth of understanding, and appreciation for his heartfelt and thoughtful answer. Then, they had only been together one week but both knew, as that sweet old lady had hoped when she bore witness to them at the café, that it was impossible for them not to fall in love as deeply and as truly as they would, as if that was written for them by those three favourite Poets.

The evening of Ed's birthday, after the presents opened and gratefully admired, once the elegant meal had been made and eaten, the expensive red wines unfastened and drunk, the two of them sat close together in the middle of the couch, finishing the last few mouthfuls of strong, bitter coffee, staring at each other with a longing from what was next assumed. Ed picked up his new gift, perched so gently on the folded wrapping beneath it, and with the tones of his beloved jazz melting softly into the background he searched the pages for the piece he most wanted to say.

Those youthful times at school and university where he had no sexual prowess or flirtatious knowledge of his own to refer, he wished he had known about borrowing the words of a genius other, one who was always better at saying things he felt but couldn't effortlessly articulate.

Although, maybe it was only because of the woman he was quoting them for was why it worked. That it was her joint enthusiasm for the borrowing of glory, the mutual admiration for such perfection of phrase that made this idea so complete.

Ed found the poem on page nine. It had fourteen lines in cummings' usual lack of customary grammar and punctuation. The deliberate form the poet had used meant Ed could translate the intentions more clearly, those urgent, breathy desires that appeared from the shapes of the wording as clear as stage directions for a play. It took Ed only a few quiet minutes to learn the whole verse by heart. He was now able to place the paperback carefully down back onto its folded brown packaging and lean in towards Izzy, his brain alert and determined, his eyes seeking deeply into hers.

"i like my body when it is with your body. It is so quite a new thing." Ed began, his soft mouth speaking the words only slightly more than a whisper. His lips brushing her own as he began opening her to kiss her but pulled back.

Izzy remembered the poem from her initial looking through of the purchased book but was unable to recall every part. Hearing him tell her these erotic promises made her breath become light as her eyes closed slightly with the lustful stirring she could feel within her.

"Muscles better and nerves more. i like your body. i like what it does i like its hows. i like to feel the spine of your body and its bones," Ed continued. His large, safe hand moving down to the end of Izzy's dress, fingers opening as he slowly walked them under the fabric and continued upwards. She parted her legs as to allow easier access, her lifting thighs giving permission to what was still to happen.

"and the trembling-firm-smooth ness and which I will again and again and again kiss," he muttered across her flushed neck, lightly caressing her shoulders, his tongue tenderly licking the base of her earlobe the same time his forefinger found the top of her panties and pressed upon it, causing Izzy to gasp involuntarily. Her wetness below was noticed as his hand carefully pulled aside the lace and moved inside to find the bud and folds of her. She tensed as his talking became hypnotic, those tender chosen letters, each delicate subtle word. She felt an intense fiery craving for him to continue, to keep touching her mind, body and soul.

"i like kissing this and that of you i like, slowly stroking the, shocking fuzz of your electric fur," he murmured over her mouth as he kissed her hard now, their tongues twisting into each other, pausing the poem yet his fingers rotated upon her smooth slickness, that sexual dampness that eased his movements with its lubricant to a faster and more frenetic pace. Her internal muscles were enflamed and engorged with the heat of such desire surging through them, alert and charged to the point of explosion.

"and what-is-it comes over parting flesh...."

"Ohhhh" Iz hummed, her breathing shallow and fractured. Her mind outside of her control as she gave herself completely to the sensations it had started throbbing from the very toes of her and crept up towards her centre, achingly slowly but purposely growing.

"Aaahhh…" she continued as the moan released from her reddened lips unable to stop it even if she'd wished.

"And eyes big love-crumbs," He whispered. Ed's fingers reached the point now when he could feel on his skin by the workings of his own hand, her body jolt and buck against him, her soft, wet hole clasp and unclench itself in rhythmic waves of release. "and possibly I like the thrill." He completed speaking into her hair as she curled into him and Ed held her close for those precious perfect minutes.

As Iz awoke from her after-state of pleasure, her big green eyes looked into Ed's, he returned her gaze, smiling as he did with his own satisfaction from achieving such a wondrous response. "You. Are. Divine." She told him as her own hands took hold of his belt, unclasping the buckle, knowing his own hardness was beneath it, so exciting it had been for Ed to watch her climax.

They continued this birthday-brilliant evening together, using now their own words and phrases throughout the remaining night, into the early morning hours, eventually exhausted with everything their bodies had performed and received: Joyful and fulfilled, grateful and hopeful. Life was glorious and euphoric.

This same life had been kind to them once.

in spite of everything

which breathes and moves, since Doom

(with white longest hands

neatening each crease)

will smooth entirely our minds

-before leaving my room

i turn, and (stooping

through the morning) kiss

this pillow, dear

where our heads lived and were.

                    27, ee cummings

Chapter Forty-Six

"I thought I could describe a state; make a map of sorrow.

Sorrow, however, turns out to be not a state but a process."

A Grief Observed, C. S. Lewis

After

Wednesday 5/6

Since last Saturday morning upon waking, Izzy replaced her daily resting on the chaise longue opposite their couch with now settling in to the left side of the sofa. She curled herself up into the corner back crease like an old cat. Her legs tucked into her safe and warm. She did not feel able at the moment to stretch out and across the fabric as she once had. The light of day felt much brighter and oppressive, as if willing an action from her, pushing her forward to achieve a braveness she wasn't yet ready for. Night time colours seemed much more forgiving of plans.

That first morning five days ago, catching sight of his wife in a new place, edging ever closer to how it once was, caught Ed with such surprise he had dropped his drink onto the floor, spilling hot coffee all down his trousers and socks and splattering along the floorboards. The favourite china cup had irreparably cracked but this fact didn't register a care from him at all. His brain was so absorbed in the morning change that had occurred. Ridiculous how a few meters of space could cause such importance. Incredulous to believe that a move in proximity, however minor, reflected something, he felt, much larger indeed. As he retrieved the kitchen paper to wipe up the liquid his eyes scanned the bowl. A solitary hearing aid rested upon the recent hand written verses and he moved his gaze over to Izzy whose eyes half-closed with drowsiness.

Since that Saturday, five days ago, Izzy would be on the couch reading, reading, reading. The autobiographies that once sat there, dust covered, had been wiped clean and depleted. Those lives stories digested, their events learned and relished. Like the recent and grateful emergent of their sexual intimacy, once Izzy love of books had been re-awaked she was ferocious in catching up all those months she had lost. It was an obsession, a rich hunger and Ed was cautiously pleased.

After such hardship and desperation for the past year, Ed was unable to simply relax and enjoy the rewards from all his efforts. Watching his wife become more and more alive and aware came not with the relief and satisfaction he had expected but rather a nervousness, an age of anxiety in which he stood back awaiting the fall, expecting these strides to get bigger too far and too quick and then almost burst into failure, disappointment and retreat. And he watched with a distance. Ed observed with a gap of self-protection so hard for him it would be to feel the repeated loss of her again.

Auden's close friend, so close he had written a published poem *Talking to Myself* about, Dr Oliver Sacks was a great author himself. One who wrote about fascinating medical conditions and the psychology of human nature. Ed had collected his titles and read each one, enjoying how the writer clarified and explained such diverse and complicated disorders. He looked over to the shelves behind him, the ones he had specially built, floor to ceiling all along the wall; full to capacity with books not published by Fallon. These lists would inspire and encourage him those work times he possibly felt slightly arrogant or over-confident in his own business abilities. The work of talented others kept him on his toes and confirmed that the Literary world, as wonderful as it was, was an industry that could not be tamed or controlled.

Walking over to the wall he found the pocket of space belonging to Dr Sacks and looked at each of their spines. 'The Man Who Mistook His Wife For A Hat', 'Seeing Voices', Uncle Tungsten', 'An Anthropologist On Mars', 'Musicophilia' and the final one he owned, the one that made his earnest hope turn icy cold, 'Awakenings'. It was a tale he tried to recall in detail but the facts eluded him so swollen his thoughts were of the ending. The pain of human lost souls denied a real life, followed by the ecstasy of awakening, that miracle; new chances, fresh beginnings with dedicated, waiting families only for it all to be gradually, significantly, taken away piece by piece as the drugs stopped working. That knowledge of immunity to the very element that was maintaining their awake-ness was the cruellest of it all. Their slow, realisation of what they were steadily losing now they experienced finding it again was heart-breaking. It was a true story Ed had never forgotten and somehow he believed it followed him today like a warning, some sort of unsettling déjà vu.

Was it better to get true happiness even for a short while and suffer its ending or to not know the bliss you will ever miss? Like his Oxford Lewis, Ed could not answer that poignant and very personal question. Like his Arthur Valentine, Ed did not feel able to decide. This world he was once so sure of felt fragile and vapid. Grief after all this time could still grab him by the throat as keenly and as harsh as if it was the first hour after death of a loved one. And the challenge of grief, as he remembered so brutally feared in his reading, was not only for those who had already passed away but those who remained though not fully living. How did that work? That limbo, that un-life, how was that possible to overcome or reach some form of the ending, that part of Acceptance?

Izzy watched Ed from her seated spot. The poetry book in her hands she had been so excitingly studying now felt frozen and stiff. And the cummings poem on the page she had reached, the one that first found their three word link, its sensual, palpable, passionate prose came back to Iz's brain; one particular line in it circled round and round behind her eyes like a pop record stuck on loop.

"You are mine. You are mine. You are mine. You. Are. Mine."

And yet no matter how many times she heard it, how many echoes she thought it again and again she still wasn't sure of the answer. Or at least she was sure of her own but after it all, after everything that had happened between them, all the sadness and the silence of their days, she sat in her safe corner and watched her husband's pensive, kind face, seeing his grey, honest eyes staring away from her and was too scared to turn that statement into a question.

"You. Are. Mine?"

And those three words troubled her deep and long, boring right into the very core of her. It felt as important as breath. That answer haunted her now as much, as true and as real as that little ghost-daughter ever did.

> "…Our marriage is a drama, but no stage-play where
> what is not spoken is not thought: in our theatre
> all that I cannot syllable You will pronounce
> in acts whose *raison-d'etre* escapes me. Why secrete
> fluid when I dole, or stretch Your lips when I joy?
>
> Demands to close or open, include or eject,
> must some from Your corner, are no province of mine
> (all I have done is to provide the time-table
> of hours when You may put them): but what is Your work
> when I liberate between a glum and a frolic?
>
> For dreams I, quite irrationally, reproach You.
> All I know is that I don't choose them: if I could,

they would conform to some prosodic discipline,

mean just what they say. Whatever point nocturnal

manias make, as a poet I disapprove…"

Talking to Myself (for Oliver Sacks), W. H. Auden

Chapter Forty-Seven

"We were promised sufferings. They were part of the programme. We were even told, 'Blessed are they that mourn', and I accept it. I've got nothing that I haven't bargained for. Of course it's different when the thing happens to oneself, not to others and in reality, not imagination."

A Grief Observed, C. S. Lewis

After

Thursday 5/6

Carron's office was nicely coloured at the end of the day. She had the height of the orange street light filtering in through the window which gave her comfy conversation area feel even more welcoming and serene. Paul had left the building already at the end of his working day, so only Ed and Carron remained. Just like the old days.

They had both brought with them their pads of meticulous notes each had been working on since Monday nothing of which they had divulged before this time. They wanted to wait and focus properly on this matter without distraction or with general flippancy. This obligation was too important for that.

Two glasses of water were poured at the start of five thirty but as their considerations and deliberations went further and further in depth, by six fifteen the whiskey had been dispensed, just single measures as they needed to maintain professional clarity, but still, the intense level of conversation felt sparked and highly charged.

"So, according to the end of Chapter thirty-one, Erika and Philip now privately recognise there is an attraction between them yet neither are able to bring it up to discuss. As it is the first event they have attended together outside of the hospital ones where Hugh resides this really is a huge deal. So the questions here are why do they not talk about it? Why does he not tell her, after the close eighteen months they have had throughout Hugh's diagnosis and treatments? Should it come from Erika first because she is the married one, therefor has the marital tie to acknowledge, rather than single Philip?" Carron queried. She was referencing the correct behaviour of married versus unmarried code.

"I believe she is still unsure," Ed countered, "because Philip behaves so kindly to all of his patients, as she has witnessed over their time together, I wonder if she feels that his behaviour to her isn't more than professional sympathy. Remember this woman has been unavailable to the opposite sex for forty years so she is a virtual stranger to the subtleties of flirting or suggestion. Her confidence has been shattered, we've read how bad she feels about herself and how this new-found loneliness is shutting her in."

"Yes I see that," she admitted. "But she has lived within a large social group with their family and friends so she is not as naive as maybe first assumed. I understand she might be lacking in confidence but her feelings, both her own and what she's wishing on behalf of Philip are genuine and acknowledged by her."

"There is also the point that bothers me," Ed confessed, "that due to her dependency on her husband for all those decades, whether she is looking at Philip as a direct replacement so as to continue the expectations she knows in daily life as a partner or that she actually wants him as a person, that she would choose him because of the total man he is. Philip deserves to be recognised as a unique human being not simply a new male replacement. I'm not sure Erika has that gravity of perception for this yet."

They both took a minute to consider this angle by taking a sip of their drinks. It was silent between them while they thought, but a required and mutual one.

"Some of these answers I'm sure lie in Arthur's split way of dividing the book into five chapter blocks, representing the stages of grief." This arching of the plot has impressed Carron greatly. She always enjoyed structure by the author, respecting that process. She had a harder time with those writers that admitted following their stream of conscious. She would wince inside as they almost laughing, described their completion of the novel as having 'winged it'. Arthur's, as indeed Auden's, disciplined hard work ethic approach was certainly her preferred method.

"The previous four sections he has clearly marked out. The pathway of intention directly starting from those very first paragraphs at their anniversary breakfast, can be translated as Denial, Anger, Bargaining, Depression. This ending he has given us clearly represents the Acceptance part, but acceptance of what?"

Ed had himself enjoyed how those elements worked parallel to Valentine's story. It felt very satisfying tying up a scenario with another wider perspective.

"It can't simply be about companionship alone. There must be more to being a couple than that. To sacrifice the possibility of more, of passion and excitement and sensual love over the basic of only friendship, loyalty only because promises were made in better, healthier times is madness. Surely that isn't enough. That can't be all there is for anybody." She queried.

Ed considered this for a moment. "Yes but that doesn't represent the depth of the relationship I am talking about. It isn't the first bloom of heart-racing sex and poetic breathlessness, but the glory and celebration in the pairing of every day. The knowing somebody chose you and still chooses you every day, every single day. In knowing that there are alternatives, the grass looks greener, the temptations of other options but they rarely come as uncomplicated and as perfect as they first appear."

He felt stronger about understanding these points than he realised. Ed was pacing the room now, speaking out loud, with perhaps more volume than he intended. He was clearly agitated by the dilemma. It felt important to him to get these opinions off his chest and throw them out into the air and off the page. Ed wanted answers. He wanted to talk about every part of these three people as if making it verbal not visual, they could crack open the puzzle. This problem of the book that had been scratching his brain, eating away at his thoughts throughout days and nights, Ed needed it solved. He continued. The freedom of talking out loud to a responding other was exhilarating.

"Who's to say leaving one and replacing with another would make you better off? In fully understanding your partner as a whole being, flaws and all, no surprises or mysteries, you are conscious of all that they are. Yet if you try to pin your next plans on a new lover, there could be so much hiding beneath, so many things you do not know and perhaps not like when you do. It is a high-end risk. It is a leap of faith: To break your promise."

His voice rose and stopped. Ed sunk back down into the chair exhausted. It was coming up to the end of their two hours timeframe and he sat deflated. So much had he expounded about those important story issues and yet no answer appeared.

Carron sat quietly watching him. Her body still but her eyes and mind bright and keen. It saddened her deeply to see him suffer so. The man she had known all their years had a cost to him, a currency spent on something he was tied to that weighed heavily upon him. It was a charge he wore at the slight creases of his eyes, in the soft exhaling of a sigh as he left for the day, of the worried line in his brow that had folded more and more, if one was looking hard enough, if someone were searching for clues.

Ed composed himself, like the ever gentleman he was and got up from the chair. His wide smile concealed all she had just noticed.

"Well, let's call it a night for this today. Thank you so much for staying on. I really must get on home now."

"Of course," Carron returned to smile. "I'll carry on for next week's meeting. It will be the deadline by then, hopefully we will have reached some sort of help for Arthur." She offered, encouragingly.

"Are you ok getting back? Can I get you a taxi?" Ed asked, as he put his coat over his arm and picked up the beautiful, battered satchel on the floor between them.

"No thank you I'll be fine." She said. Her answer bothered her but she didn't want to be a burden to him too. She was more than capable to organise herself back. Her independence was something she felt that he admired in her and she wished to keep that mindful to him. He smiled. He did know. He did feel relief in only have one important woman in his life to look after that night, not to be a carer for two.

Walking out Ed remained unsettled. The world in his eyes stayed unclear. He felt he was on the verge of something imperative but also at a loss of what he should do. He kept on walking and walking. Somewhere in his bag he hoped would be a poem he could find just for him tonight: A direct verse, a marker, that constant, universal truth: One that might tell him what to do.

"I wish that there were some wing, some wing,
Under which I could hide my head,
A soft grey wing, a beautiful thing,
Oh I wish there were such a wing…"

I Wish, Stevie Smith

"And it was at that age…Poetry arrived

in search of me. I don't know, I don't know where

it came from, from winter or a river.

I don't know how or when,

no, they were not voices, they were not

words, nor silence,

but from a street I was summoned,

from the branches of night,

abruptly from the others,

among violent fires

or returning alone,

there I was without a face

and it touched me."

Pablo Neruda

Chapter Forty-Eight

"Certainty, fidelity

On the stroke of midnight pass

Like vibrations of a bell,

And fashionable madmen raise

Their pedantic boring cry:

Every farthing of the cost,

And the dreaded cards foretell,

Shall be paid, but from this night

Not a whisper, not a thought,

Nor a kiss nor look be lost."

Lullaby, W.H. Auden (part one/two)

After

Thursday 6/6

The two glasses of water sat upon the table next to two poured whiskey ones, next to the two pads of notes, next to the two of them. Carron and Ed had both been waiting for this Thursday meeting as if time has slowed to treacle. In some ways it could not arrive soon enough, in others they would have been grateful for any imposed delay.

Halfway through going over their individual comments and questions threaded into their manuscripts copies they once again came to the undecided conclusion of the book. Carron had suggested they go through the possibility of if Erika chose Philip over Hugh and how that may play out so Ed was talking this out for the characters.

"And then what? What if that too doesn't work out? What if Philip is no better or even no worse than what Erika had before? What does she do then?" Ed was questioning. Of all the characters he was struggling to get underneath Erika the most. The most pivotal part and yet the one who shoulders the future choice and its effects. "Does she leave again? Does she go back?"

"No Arthur has made it very clear that once Erika has chosen Philip there will be no reconciling with Hugh. Likewise if she chooses her husband then Philip and her can never occur again in the future, whatever Hugh's final diagnosis."

"So if Erika chose not ever to Hugh, now deciding not to stay with him will she continue to keep looking? To leave a trail of brokenness behind her whilst she seeks for something or someone that may never be right, that may never exist? Only be missing because she herself is?" He was cross at feeling so contained for her. This lack of otherness, or worse this playing with others feelings purely for her own self-need. It felt claustrophobic to be so clinically defined.

"But if she chooses Hugh and he continues to go further into his Alzheimers, she will have lost both. A horrible punishment for a woman so capable of giving and receiving affection and happiness: A life with no love reciprocated isn't enough?"

Carron gulped at the whiskey glass and breathed out loudly. So long had she been searching this question, so painful the fact. She looked up at Ed and he looked at her too. The air was hanging on all the thoughts and arguments and ideas and possibilities that had swollen this space over the past fortnight: Perhaps over much, much longer too.

He sat and he sighed. He waited just a beat to find a pathway through from the forest of fiction they had grown around themselves. A road.

"But that is not what love is." Ed whispered.

"Love isn't giving to receive. Loving someone isn't putting a price out for them to give back a fair exchange. If you love something you must love it regardless of what you get back from it or what it can do for you."

He spoke with a soft assurance, a throat that began filling with the semblance of a solution.

"Sometimes you don't get long at all. Sometimes you get a whole lifetime. But does that mean that the ones who have a shorter time, by no fault of their own, have less worth or value? Is it not always the unknown, that despite the unknown, that we must continue to hope and persist because we wish for more, for extra, for longer. It is the very fact that we do not want it to end, ever, even if we have had our entire lives with the person we love, even if you both met at sixteen and then lived till a hundred together; the first one to die, or forget or be lost, even after eighty-four years the other would say, "I am heart-broken. I am cheated. I wish more than anything that we could have more time.""

"But what if there is nothing left of the person you once loved? What if they are in a coma or brain damaged to the point of no emotional return? How do you decide to remain because of the person they were but can never be again? How do you reach the point to stay despite them offering no hope or expectation? Is that all you accept from life? Is that what you do?" Carron asked back. Her eyes stinging as she spoke as she tried to push the hot tears back.

"Is that what I do?" Ed asked slowly, as if the question was for himself to Carron, instead of Erika. And those five words hung in the air between them like a guillotine's blade, its polished sharpened edge shining on the night-bulb like a warning siren light.

Ed looked at Carron and she returned his gaze. She did not seem to be moving. Her chest appeared to not rise and fall with any breaths, so tense was the room they shared.

"I want you to live." She whispered: A confession that was as weighted as if she told him to kiss her. She had decided on her ending for the three characters. She always had.

Ed looked at the two piles of notes on the table beside Carron. One was the outlines for Erika leaving with Philip and the other was Erika remaining with Hugh. Both felt valid and understandable. But this was a decision that had its time limit now. No more hours or days could be spent going back and forth on the values and virtues each had addressed.

Arthur bloody Valentine, how Ed hated him at that moment: Had he known what his asking would cause? Had he seen this circumstance, as close as he has known everyone involved, inside and outside of this office all along?

It was time for a choice. There was no way out of this now, too much had been said. A possibility opened up that could never be shut back down quiet again, folded into a box like a secret. It was time for a choice. It was time for Acceptance, whatever and whoever that may be. It was time for the ever after.

> "Beauty, midnight, vision dies:
> Let the winds of dawn that blow
> Softly round your dreaming head
> Such a day of sweetness show
> Eye and knocking heart may bless,
> Find the mortal world enough;
> Noons of dryness see you fed
> By the involuntary powers,
> Nights of insult let you pass
> Watched by every human love."

Lullaby, W.H. Auden (part two/two)

Chapter Forty-Nine

"...for poetry makes nothing happen; it survives

In the valley of its making where executives

Would never want to tamper, flows on south

From ranches of isolation and the busy griefs,

Raw towns that we believe and die in; it survives

A way of happening, a mouth."

In Memory of W. B. Yeats, W. H. Auden

After

Marcus Hollier was aware that he had only five minutes left on this interview. The organisers were incredibly strict on times as they had so many other events tightly packed in over these three days. Same premises re-used and converted to host another celebrated speaker or to create a workshop space to those new waiting audiences. The crowd seated around them had been admirably entertained. Their ticket prices justified and Marcus felt sure that his part in the opening of this monumental anniversary was work well done.

A few weeks prior to that day, Marcus had emailed over the list of questions he had planned to ask Ed, to give him the chance to work through his answers, add or make comments on anything he felt of importance or remove any particular lines of enquiry he felt uncomfortable with.

In that small gap of time between Ed's last answer and this final question Marcus stared across at the man who had been so generous to him over the years, his inspiration and teacher, both in their literary world and in his own life. That admired mentor who a few years before stayed up for weeks with him when Marcus was finalising his first award winning book; that thoughtful friend who had sent him a copy of Rainer Maria Rilke's 'Love Song' when Marcus remained baffled with what to choose to propose to his future wife; the gentle man who took the seat behind him in church, when Marcus's own father died, a strong hand on his shoulder when he himself did not know if he was able to complete the eulogy he had written to say.

"You have talked us through here tonight, your thoughts on Talk versus Speech, on Speech versus Books and finally on Poetry above all others. It really has been a great honour to have you share these with us all." Ed smiled over at him as Marcus continued. "My final question is that you mentioned earlier that phrase 'Words can save your life...' could you perhaps expand on this idea?"

Still after almost this whole hour long, the entire audience was soundless. Their faces had been leaning inwards towards these two speakers to catch each answer Ed divulged. All were aware that the time here was nearly over and they each very much wanted to hear this final part.

"Of course," Ed began slowly. He was ready to tackle this question. He knew that Marcus had cleverly architected the direction of this interview so as to lead up to climax the talk at such an extreme statement.

Ed had spent years with this answer burning within him. He had analysed, talked through, queried, listened, trialled and faltered many times, since that first day in his tiny toddler hands held up a simple picture book. It was his life's theory and his own very tragic personal experience that set him up for such a test of it. Putting his opinion in such an absolute belief would inevitably set him up for a variety of arguments against, definite disagreements and a possible backlash of him as a person as a whole, but he had to be true to himself and he had reached a time in his life where he was comfortable with the honesty that embodied his years in work, and all that which spilt over it into more private situations. It was true *for* him therefore it was true *to* him. He hoped others would be generous enough to see it so.

"Over the decades I have been living on this incredible, perfectly imperfect planet, almost all of it has included in no small way, the use of language, books, communications, prose, cards, letters, signing and more.

I have surrounded my adult life for both career and pleasure in a business of Literature, thousands upon thousands of collected works. I immersed myself in the absolute glory of writings in fiction, non-fiction, verse, every font and script, paper weight, size, shape, colour and finish. I have read and I have learnt, my goodness, I have learnt.

When I extoll such an outrageous statement as to the possibility of words saving lives it is simply because I not only believe it whole heartedly through my love and theory of its potential power but I have lived it, seen it with my own eyes, in my own life, the reality of what they can achieve when all other options seemed to fail.

I am not alone in having experienced a heart-breaking situation. No one who has truly lived can have done so without disaster and misfortune, calamity or catastrophe touching them at some, if not many times over their years.

For my own situation I found myself completely out of my depth, as if off in the middle of the ocean storm with no oars or life jacket, no island on the horizon or hope of rescue. I was unable to help the very person I wished to protect most in the world and it was, for me, the very worst thing imaginable.

As someone who puts great stock in studying for answers, finding a resource to solve new dilemmas, I was suddenly bereft of all practical fixes. I was doing the correct things physically, saying the recommended phrases verbally, believing in what it all meant, but none of this could break through to the real depth of the problem. It didn't manage to fix the root of the pain.

Time being a great healer platitude whilst may surely be useful to some situations made my own one more of a worry. The longer it was taking to solve, the further away the chance of recovery was becoming. I was utterly helpless. I felt for the first time as a grown man, completely without the ability to affect the outcome my own life, to ensure my own desired future."

"That sounds terrifying." Marcus noted solemnly, siding his head towards his shoulder in a gesture of care. Ed smiled back. He knew Marcus was aware of lots of his past but this particular subject was one they had never together discussed. Some things, even to people close to you, remain out of bounds.

Ed was interested in raising this personal perspective up now only because he had enough time to distance himself from it and his considerate brain was curious as to understand what happened to Izzy and him sixteen years ago. It was at first purely a thoughtful exercise, an intelligent exploration and yet it now seemed to him something that underpinned the absolute essence of his very self. His actions had depended on his own history and experiences and the outcome he created was due to who he was: The two things he absolutely loved most in the world became the perfect solution for both.

"When I say 'Words Can Save Your Life' I suppose I mean is that words have saved my life in that they have given me back a life I thought was gone. Saved as in resuscitated, lost as in out of reach whose tethered rope is out of sight and you're not sure you can ever find it. All of this is discussed fully in the book 'Wystan's Words' which in itself is probable banishment from the clandestine society we created so very long ago, right here in Oxford.

But I found that words, specifically through poems, and actually in the performance of reading them out loud, for Auden always insisted poetry was a verbal art; speaking from one person to another, doing this awoke a part of self that would otherwise, I felt, remain forever broken.

And it comes back round again to that beautiful word a 'soul'. For me that means whatever a person is, their originality, their heart's own heart, that part of them that reaches a sense of peace and purpose with who they are on this earth: invisible even to atoms."

At this part Ed looked to be faltering, taking a breath to follow up what he was meaning to say. Looking out to the left of him, in the blur of the many, to try and focus on his last part.

"I lost my child, our baby daughter. This loss took my wife away from me. I did not know if I would ever get her back. I wanted them both but of course it was only possible to have one. After that happened I would describe my wife then as being a body without a soul, a hollow frame. The soul that was missing, that true essential self was gone, perhaps for always. But I didn't want that to be our story. I would never let a book I had loved so much end in such a way. I needed to try and find that soul to save her life, and in doing so, also save my own.

And I followed the truth told by Jim Harrison who said that 'Poetry, at its best, is the language your soul would speak, if you could teach your soul to speak.' So that was what I did. I found that voice from the poems of so many others and I put my faith, my own desperate conviction, into this belief: This possibility, this Hope, that perched soul bird. Grief, true grief, for any person can be such an infinite fracture you see, that chasm of damage. And what else did I know how to do."

He became aware that the people around him might now want to know the outcome of his personal life, those who had not read his book about it all. *"Did it work? Did she come back to you?"* he could imagine them waiting to hear. Ed looked over to Marcus at this point, feeling a little fragile. Marcus in turn picked up a copy of "Wysten's Words" that had been resting against the chair leg this entire time. Raising it up for the crowds, they each grinned at how this noiselessly showed the way to reach that answer. Feeling slightly relieved at how Marcus had diffused the situation, Ed sighed out a little, wishing now for this interview over.

They both knew that time was nearly up and Ed hoped he had represented himself well. He was never one for showy parades or flashes of own ego, without this book to promote, or notion to explore, he was intrinsically a very private man.

He wondered if she minded how he had phrased everything. Would she have thought it too indiscreet? Would she have been upset he had discussed their worst of times this way? The pain of that time weighed heavy on his chest with the memory of it all and his heart felt as if it was hurting all over again. He had seen the prepared questions and knew it wasn't on the list but still that remembrance of Frost's two roads choices and outcomes "….*And what about your wife?*"

"So you believe poems still matter, they are life-saving even; for our day-to-day, the important situations, those most frightening or loving times. Having explained to us how vital feel the work of Poets are, can you please expand on your new project for them." Marcus asked.

"Certainly, thank you. With the backing of the Education Council, Advertising Campaigns and Government schemes we are introducing a new arena for Poets and their work. The charity at Fallon House Publishing will create a new department to welcome writings from across the country, available to all ages, backgrounds and abilities. The plan is to incorporate the art of poetry back into the everyday masses, to become an inclusion with the modern world, not just thought of as a dated genre of literature only available or understood by a select few.

The hope is to find new fresh voices and discover insights into our individual journeys and opinions that can resonate and connect to us all. It's time, I believe, to elevate this art into the mainstream and give it a respected profile that can be enjoyed by so many more."

"This new project, the scheme 'Poetry Always' it is called, to any potential bards that might be here tonight, any future verse writers amongst us, how would you explain to them what their role is? What can best describe that duty of a poet?" Marcus enquired.

Ed paused for a second and slowly picked up the book that had been resting on the chair arm for the duration of the hour and carefully pulled his reading glasses from his top jacket pocket.

The stage seemed small, the light now singular, spotlight on him only and it meant he could not see the seated crowds around. Ed continued, responding to this final important question. "If you will permit me to answer that with one of my favourite Poets to another, written by a man much greater at this language than I...

...Follow, poet, follow right

To the bottom of the night,

With your unconstraining voice

Still persuade us to rejoice;

With the farming of the verse

Make a vineyard of the curse,

Sing of human unsuccess

In a rapture of distress;

In the deserts of the heart

Let the healing fountain start,

In the prison of his days

Teach the free man how to praise."

Silence filled the enormous Sheldonian Theatre space. Not a cough nor a shuffle of pages, no feet pressed upon the ground ready to leave. Just the still air in the semi-dark as Ed sat on that stage, underneath the clouds and Angels painted ceiling, his chair down from the exquisitely carved wooden columns and apexes, all hundreds of years old and would, he hoped, remain for many hundreds still.

This same esteemed hall where they had snuck in all those decades ago, through the side street courtyard, easily twisting open the small copper locks in the centre of the huge heavy oak, inlaid doors. This reverential space which housed the group of shy, up and coming under graduates ready to discuss, argue, listen, learn and discover that secret they were searching for almost forty years before. They all stood around him like spirits, hovering about as he spoke of what they spent their whole shared knowledge uncovering.

Lost in his private memories Ed took a few seconds to notice the noise that raised around him, its thunder and banging. He removed his reading glasses and looked up to see a thousand people in all corners of the room, standing and clapping ferociously. Some were crying, others were nodding, a few cheering, all were smiling towards him in their own way, lifted and grateful at their hour hearing from this great man; this generous and insightful gentleman, them all now Aslans by default.

Marcus reached over towards his revered guest, his friend, and shook his hand warmly and powerfully, so very touched he had been a part of this important evening. The loud applause crackled on.

Behind Marcus Hollier's shoulder, along from the Bookseller's desk just off left stage, Ed looked over, his eyes adjusting to the up surging lights. He struggled a little but then caught sight of the three people he most wanted to be standing nearby. There stood two strapping teenage boys dressed in their typical blue jeans and comfortable hoodies, one pale featured, handsomely freckled and one much darker with wider grey eyes. Both stood tall and broad, thin but not skinny, identical grins flashing across their ever so-familiar faces as their arms crashed together, clapping the loudest of all.

In between them, dwarfed by these two almost-men, was a dark haired woman; her bright green eyes sparkling, her long wavy hair down but clipped up at the temples, showing a streak of silvery grey that denoted her age.

Her clapping was strong.

Her clapping was proud and full of life and love.

Her clapping's pace matched the exact beat of his own heart.

"…And down by the brimming river
I heard a lover sing
Under an arch of the railway:
'Love has no ending.

I love you dear, I'll love you
Till China and Africa meet,
And the river jumps over the mountain
And the salmon sing in the street,

'I'll love you till the ocean
Is folded and hung out to dry
And the seven stars go squawking
Like geese about the sky.

The years shall run like Rabbits,

For in my arms I hold

The Flowers of the Ages,

And the first love of the world..."

As I Walked Out One Evening, W. H. Auden

Chapter Fifty

"love is the voice under all silences, the hope which has no opposite in fear;

the strength so strong mere force is feebleness:

the truth more first than sun, more last than star."

ee cummings

After

Thursday 6/6 – 2pm

Dearest daughter of mine,

I'm so sorry to have to write this but I know of no other way to do it. I am afraid I must leave you here now. I feel strongly enough that your Grandparents, who went many years ago where I hope you are going, will look after you until we meet again. They are such caring people I absolutely know you will like them. I think they must so much miss having a daughter to take care of. You can't know the joy of being united with you will give them.

I wish I could describe how wonderful it has been to spend this time with you, your spirit, your soul, all the enduring love we had for you that got left behind when you were not able to live. I have adored being your Mother and am grateful you managed to stay with me for as long as we had. There is still so much I want to tell you and teach you, to show you and hold you. I think I always will want that, but I must be at peace with doing what I could with the time that was given.

Half-living between two worlds, whilst necessary for me for that time, I understand is no real living, not forever, and so I must go and get back to your Father, live the life I had created for myself before. It is a true heart-break of mine that he never knew you the way I did but I am in no doubt he would have been an exceptional parent. If I did anything right ever it is that I chose him very well.

He has been so endlessly kind to me, so very good to let me be with you but it is him who needs me now and I have been away too long. I dearly hope I have not left it too late.

If we are ever lucky enough to have a child again I want to say that I know this can never replace you or you be returned through them. You are your own star, however brief you burned among us. Know you will shine on always in our sky.

I will think of you still, every day, every single day. You have been without question, the greatest thing I have ever made. I wish you happiness and light. I wish that you feel every piece of the love we have for you and it carries you through to wherever you now may be, whatever you now may do.

I can't bear to say the word Goodbye to you, so perhaps you will allow me to simply write Goodnight.

Your loving Mum,

Izzy xxx

She had taken the paper from their bureau to use for her letter and borrowed Ed's fountain pen lying on the coffee table, to write her words. Izzy handwriting appeared slightly faint and weak, such as she was not used to activity of most kinds. Her penmanship, though light in touch was deep in meaning, and it gave the cream sheet a look of fine beauty and loving care.

Once she had waited a minute for the ink to dry, Izzy picked up the two hearing aids from the grey bowl and gently placed them inside her ear canals, activating them as she did so. She carefully placed her letter on the top of the pile of poems, almost fifty of them there, and returned to her favoured seat.

She did not want to look out of the window anymore. The skyline view was foggy and distant. Instead she pulled at the soft blue blanket, tucking herself straight on the long chair so she could see up at the pale, blank ceiling. Izzy's head rested back on the centre of her cotton cushion, both ears uncovered and alert. Her eyes seeing the room's details as they truly were, no longer through that muted reflected glass. Sharp colours and subtle tones amazed her, each puff and squeak of the old radiators, every whirl and tap of the branches knocking against the lamppost outside their front door below, were delivered clearly and keenly, filtering through the plastic pearls in her ears, waking up her old life.

The glass bird smiled to itself for the very first time. It felt dizzy with care and exhaustion. The start of the dark, dense longings that it had kept so securely inside began leaking out as smoke, trailing away invisibly and gratefully like small, perfect clouds. The string above it was threadbare now. The full weight of what it had to support for so long had worn it down to the point of such weakness that it could not hold the glass steady whilst the bitter vapours seeped off, unseen by those beneath. The glass pulled against it with the motion of emptying as the wire started to loosen and give; tired the bird was, so very tired.   That worn wire helplessly and inevitably snapped.

"No wonder then so many die of grief,
So many are so lonely as they die;
No one has yet believed or like a lie:
Another time has other lives to live.

Another Time, W. H. Auden

Chapter Fifty-One

"You can't see anything properly when your eyes are blurred with tears. You can't, in most things, get what you want if you want it too desperately: anyway, you can't get the best out of it."
A Grief Observed, C. S. Lewis

After

Friday 6/6

Fallon House Internal Email

To: Ed Williams   From: Carron Larkin

Re: Resignation

Dear Ed,

So it has come to this time which was always a possibility, that I would be leaving my post at Fallon for a job at another Publishing House. I have accepted Hank's offer to run his Scotland Offices in Edinburgh as of next month. As per my contract I am obliged to give four weeks' notice but as I am going to what could be considered a rival company, I will assume I take this as 'Gardener's Leave'.

I have organised my desk with all the relevant files and list of Authors alongside their up to date information and future project plans. The company laptop remains there also and it's passwords to access my emails and folders on it, I have left in the top right drawer.

It has truly been a remarkable journey for me to have helped start this business from the ground up and I take with me many years of happy memories and invaluable knowledge and experience in this industry we both so admire.

I do wish you and Isobel the very best with your future plans and life together. There's nothing else to say on this personal note except I heard a while back about your poetry plan with your old College friends and I thought it was indeed wonderful. I had been waiting maybe to have been asked to contribute but that offer never came forth. Perhaps this was for the best. Poetry can, even without realising it by the chooser, be sometimes too truthful to bear.

I'm not sure when we might meet up again. No doubt our paths will cross over the years with some of the bigger work events and ceremonies. It will be strange after so long to not be in contact as we are used to. Again, maybe this will be a good thing for us all. For many years I have clung to waiting for a life that didn't belong to me. So now I am using this change to initiate the start of brand new chances and I am hopeful for great things.

In the spirit of a final farewell, all confessionals disclosed, nothing lost or forgotten, I would like to end not with my own words but with a shared other. You will of course recognise it. You might well have always known it. That man always could say with his understated honesty the things I, and so many others in life, struggle to voice.

Thank you for the past years. Here's to mutual and future successes. Please send on my farewells to Arthur Valentine. He was always the maker of the pair of us at Fallon, I never thought it would be through him it would end us too.

Goodbye Edward.

C

The More Loving One

Looking up at the stars, I know quite well

That, for all they care, I can go to hell,

But on earth indifference is the least

We have to dread from man or beast.

How should we like it were stars to burn

With a passion for us we could not return?

If equal affection cannot be,

Let the more loving one be me.

Admirer as I think I am

Of stars who do not give a damn,

I cannot now I see them, say

I missed one terribly all day.

Were all stars to disappear or die

I should learn to look up at an empty sky

And feel its total dark sublime,

Though this might take a little time.

W. H. Auden

Chapter Fifty-Two

"I think I am beginning to understand why grief feels like suspense..."
A Grief Observed, C. S. Lewis

After

It was time. After all the hard work that glass bird had done: It had watched and wished. It had held and hoped. So full it had been; so much hidden tight inside. It heard silences so loud that they filled each room in the entire house. It had listened to a lone voice talking words written from lives extinguished centuries ago to spark a life's future yet to be found.

That bird's obligation above had ended and its spirit let out its final sigh, long and heavy, released from duty and ready to leave its post. The un-noticed soul wished it could fly now to a place where that child went. It would have been lovely to stay with her again after such a journey.

The dark, endless hole it had swung over since the day it was made, remained beneath still. It always had been there, waiting.

The bird was sad for its wire's hold to be ending however hard it tried to remember with pride all those broken-hearted evenings and disappeared-days they managed to stay so strong for.

It would see no more what lay below, its eyes had been closed for almost a week now as it gave itself up to the tiredness within. With a slight snap and ping that was so inaudible not one speck of dust lifted or air flow trembled, the bird fell, taking with it most of the clear strand tied to the ridge in its back.

Falling.

Falling.

Light as pale dandelion downs.

Quiet as forgetting.

Falling.

BUMP.   Stop.

The tiny bird shuddered awake, surprised at this pause. It could feel its delicate shell was

horizontal now. It was lying on its side, weightless and supported. Its glass was unbroken.

The floor beneath was soft and smooth. The bird felt anxious. It had resigned itself

to being lost forever in the darkness, always floating down, no touch or notice. Its sorrow

acknowledged and fate accepted. It did not want false comfort or delay. Carefully it peered

out to check this foundation, to see what had so far halted the plan.

Creams, whites, shade of beiges and pastel blues, some softer and cleanly ironed flat,

others spongy with tiny fragments of pulped edges pressed together tight, like molecules,

fixed to make a rectangle form. Each different size and weight connected together as a

quilt. Layers upon layers to garner it strength; a bonding of fine structures placed upon

another to create a singular harmonious force.

Upon these lightly coloured pieces it could see lines and shapes of all loops, dots and curves. Some Pollack-splattered with treacle opaque pools, some sea blue stains carving deep ridges with care, others the velvet of ash markings above the white background with its granite point: Every part different, each adding together.

The bird was confused as it rocked itself upright. What was this land? Why had it stopped?

Enveloped gently all around it were sheets and pages and papers and notes. Every poem written down, every single piece that was chosen by them and for them in their hours of need was placed there, keeping that bird safe, like a nest. The sheets filled up that dark, lost hole that seemed so fearful and endless. They filled it to the brim and above, an outpouring of stories, a disclosure of The Secret.

And the abyss had changed from what felt like the darkest of black shades to a more shadowy, lighter film. It wasn't endless at all now. It had a smaller, round circumference and a low curved base to hold everything in. It was solid, yet splintered in parts but these had been tenderly repaired. It was hand built and coated in a perfect varnish of glossy grey.

The exhausted bird raised a last beautiful smile and slowly lay itself back down for its final sleep, settled, thankful, silent and at peace.

"… 'Then I am your servant and no more your master. The cure of death is dying.
He who lays down his liberty in that act receives it back.'…"
The Pilgrim's Progress, C. S. Lewis

Afterward

kintsukuroi

(n) (v. phr.) "to repair with gold" the art of repairing pottery with gold or silver lacquer and understanding that the piece is more beautiful for having been broken.

Printed in Great
Britain
by Amazon

32016461R00161